NORGIL
The Magician

NORGIL
The Magician

Maxwell Grant

1977
The Mysterious Press
New York

NORGIL THE MAGICIAN

Published by arrangement with The Condé Nast Publications Inc.

Copyright © 1937, 1938, 1940 by Street & Smith Publications, Inc.

Copyright renewed © 1965, 1966, 1968, by The Condé Nast Publications Inc.

New material copyright © 1977 by The Mysterious Press

These stories originally appeared in the following publications:

"Norgil—Magician" in *Crime Busters*, Nov. 1937
"Ring of Death" in *Crime Busters*, Jan. 1938
"Murderer's Throne" in *Crime Busters*, Feb. 1938
"The Second Double" in *Crime Busters*, March 1938
"Drinks on the House" in *Crime Busters*, April 1938
"Chinaman's Chance" in *Crime Busters*, May 1938
"The Glass Box" in *Crime Busters*, June 1938
"Battle of Magic" in *Mystery Magazine*, July 1940

SECOND PRINTING BEFORE PUBLICATION

ISBN 0-89296-031-0 Trade edition
ISBN 0-89296-032-9 Limited edition

Library of Congress Catalogue Card Number 76-16891

Printed in the United States of America

The Mysterious Press
P.O. Box 334
East Station
Yonkers, N.Y. 10704

To
Jay Marshall—
An inspiration then
And now

Contents

Introduction

MAGIC AND MYSTERY are so closely interwoven that it is hard to tell where one leaves off and the other begins, or vice versa. From the literary standpoint, this makes it very difficult to blend the two, without favoring one at the expense of the other. Perhaps the most pressing problem was how to balance fact against fiction, since the slightest shift of weight in the wrong direction could teeter the whole works into a landslide. Professional magicians themselves were faced by this dilemma, back at the turn of the century, a most notable example being that of Harry Kellar, who took over as America's leading magician following the demise of Herrmann the Great in 1896.

Kellar advertised his show with huge lithographs depicting him surrounded by devils ranging in size from a full-fledged Mephistopheles down to lesser imps who perched on his shoulder or sat at his feet, poring over books of magic. These had a two-way effect upon the general public. In large cities, many customers were attracted to the theater actually expecting to see some of Kellar's satanic assistants, while in smaller towns, many people shunned the show, rather than come under the baneful influence of the Evil One.

When Howard Thurston took over the Kellar show in 1908, he continued to advertise his hellish helpers to such an extent that he practically established them as a trademark, but gradually they went out of vogue. Still, Thurston continued to feature Kellar's "spirit cabinet" in which ghostly manifestations transpired, much to the amazement of American audiences, while the Great Raymond, during a series of world tours, presented his "Trip to Spookville" in nearly every country that he visited.

The biographies of earlier magicians had been so well garnished with fictional touches that it was inevitable that their modern successors should waver between fact and fantasy when recounting their adventures. I was fortunate enough to become involved in both phases of this trend during the 1920's. When Houdini switched from vaudeville to appear in movie thrillers during the era of the silent screen, he called upon the now famous fantasy writer, H.P. Lovecraft, to "ghost" some incredible adventures for *Weird Tales,* one being a first-hand account of a night that Houdini allegedly spent deep in the Great Pyramid of Egypt. A few years later, when Houdini abandoned his brief movie career to take out a full evening magic show, he deputized me to describe his most dangerous true life escapes, which I had just completed at the time of his death on October 31, 1926, and which were published soon afterward as Houdini's last interview.

With Thurston, it was a continuous seesaw between fact and fancy. After working with him on factual articles for the *Saturday Evening Post* in 1925, we switched to fictional adventures in lesser magazines during 1927; then, during the summer of 1928, I helped him complete his autobiography,

which I immediately sold to *Collier's* and arranged for its
further publication in book form under the title of *My Life
in Magic*. By 1930, I was doing Thurston scripts for a pro-
posed radio show, again with fiction in the ascendant, but
the project was postponed when Thurston signed a year's
contract for a children's radio show. Having a year to spare,
I took up mystery writing on my own and developed a
character called The Shadow, whose fictional adventures,
appearing in a magazine of the same title, were to keep me
considerably occupied for nearly twenty years, during which
period I turned out 282 Shadow novels under the pen name
of Maxwell Grant.

My backlog of magical experience was helpful in creating
both situations and devices for The Shadow, who frequently
vanished from the midst of attacking crooks or arrived
suddenly from nowhere to wreak vengeance on evil-doers.
He also specialized in quick changes, discarding his black
cloak and slouch hat to assume the role of Lamont Cranston,
a debonair club man, or to appear in some other guise that
suited his immediate need. But often, as I applied those
touches, my thoughts reverted to the possibilities of a magician detective who would be confronted with situations that
could only be resolved by using his own devices.

From long and continued association with many professional magicians, I felt that the best way to involve such a
character in a mystery story or a crime case was to precipitate
him into the midst of it and have him wangle his way out in
truly magical fashion. Treated from a backstage angle, this
offered a wide range of intriguing prospects that could be
built into a series of novels, particularly as the world of
magic was itself undergoing a decided change in the early
1930's. The era of the big show was over, except for occasional revivals, since talking pictures had usurped the place of
the legitimate theater. Vaudeville was on the wane for the

same reason, with hour-long presentations of magic supplanting the shorter specialty acts. Those performers, however, had found new fields in night clubs and on cruise ships, as well as private engagements which even included appearances at the White House.

In the field of mystery writing, new characters were continually cropping up, particularly in popular magazines, where The Shadow had set the pace, so the time seemed ripe indeed for a fictional magician who could switch from one type of show to another and mingle mystery in with mystification. When I suggested it to John Nanovic, who edited *The Shadow Magazine,* he liked the idea and took it up with H. W. Ralston, the general manager of Street & Smith Publications. It was approved as a future prospect, but the question arose just where to put it.

Character magazines were already in abundance, with others in the planning stage, which meant that my magician-detective would have to await his turn, if it ever came at all. The big hitch, as Mr. Ralston put it, was that there was less than a fifty-fifty chance that a new character would gain sufficient readership to show a profit, so until someone devised a way of testing popular appeal, it was better to hold off than risk the loss of the initial investment. By the next time we met, I had found what I thought was an answer to that problem and I expressed it.

With the average character magazine of *The Shadow's* type, the trend was to cut the lead novel to about half the length of the magazine, filling the remaining pages with short stories. Why not carry that trend still further, by reducing the novel to one-third, eliminating the shorts entirely and replacing them with two other novels, each involving a different character? This would give the reader three novels for the price of one, a bargain that many buyers would find hard to resist. Not only would that increase the magazine's chance for success, it would serve as a proving ground to test the popularity of new characters. By polling the opinions of readers, the character who proved most popular could be promoted to a magazine of his own and a newcomer could be introduced to replace him.

That was early in 1936, just five years after I had written my first Shadow novel. In the fall, the first Shadow radio show went on the air, featuring Lamont Cranston with other personages from the magazine stories, and proved an immediate success. That spurred a new demand for more character novels and early in 1937, Street & Smith launched the new magazine that I had suggested under the title of *Crime Busters,* but instead of featuring three novel-length stories, they ran eight—and later nine—novelettes. That was good policy as they had the writers available and it enabled them to get the new magazine under way without delay.

I was called on for a magician story for the first issue, so I gave my character the name of Norgil, which he formed by juggling the letters of his actual name, which was Loring. He also could change it into Ling Ro, a title which he used when called upon to perform wizardry in Chinese costume. Since The Shadow's popularity was at a peak and Street & Smith had earlier contracted to take my entire output of mystery fiction, I used my pen name of Maxwell Grant with the Norgil stories as well, partly on the assumption that it would help the sale of *Crime Busters,* which it may have, for the new magazine sold well from the start. Later its title was changed to *Mystery Magazine* and it continued until the paper shortage of World War II led to its suspension.

As originally planned, readers' opinions of the various characters were requested from the start and the Norgil stories stood high enough in the rating to have warranted a magazine of their own, if that proposal had been carried through. So it is quite appropriate that this selection of

Norgil stories should appear in a single volume after a lapse of nearly forty years, particularly at a time when a new wave of interest in magic and magicians may cause present-day readers to revel in the ways and wiles of the wizards who flourished way back then. For Norgil, along with most of the people who worked with him, had their counterparts in real life, as some who remember those days can testify.

Norgil, himself, had so many prototypes that many of his stories suggested themselves automatically. Like Blackstone or Calvert, both headliners at the time, he could switch from fifty-minute shows at movie houses to a full evening extravaganza, with an enlarged company. He also had a counterpart in Russell Swann, who played de luxe hotels in New York, Washington, San Francisco, and even London. That put him into society circles and lecture circuits like Dunninger, the mind reader, and Dr. Harlan Tarbell, author of a famous magic course.

Norgil's occasional switch to the character of Ling Ro was inspired by George Reuschling, who did a Chinese act under the name of Rush Ling Toy and also doubled in a quick-change act—often on the same program!—as Lafollette, the Man of Many Faces. Nor was Norgil averse to donning Hindu robes and appearing as a Hindu mystic like Rajah Raboid; and when occasion demanded he could stage a midnight spook show, rivaling the real-life Doctor Neff, whose Madhouse of Mystery teemed with ghosts galore.

Like Houdini, Norgil would frequently bring business to the theater by doing an overboard box escape from the bottom of a river, but despite all that, I had still greater plans for Norgil. I hoped to send him on a world tour, emulating such Greats as Raymond and Carter, but that time never came. Instead, I kept him in the U.S.A., where he frequently was seen at magical conventions as a shining example for such future wonder workers as Mark Wilson and Doug Henning.

One final note: Some critics have felt that Norgil was a trifle lax in his choice of a stage name, as there can be confusion as to its correct pronunciation, the "g" being soft as in "forge," not hard as in "morgue." They should be reminded that the Great Houdini was caught in the same bind when he borrowed the name of a French *prestidigitateur,* Robert-Houdin, and added an "i" to it. For a time, some people insisted on calling him "Hoo-dan-eye" instead of "Hoo-dee-knee," but his fame increased to the point where everyone eventually came to his way of thinking.

Let's hope that the same rule will apply with Norgil.

When you think of magic, think of Norgil. The "g" is the same in both, just as the "G" in Gibson is the same as in Grant.

—Walter Gibson

NORGIL
The Magician

Norgil—Magician

Chapter I
THE GHOST THAT WASN'T

THE ORCHESTRA FINISHED with a crash, as the girl stepped from the front of the huge, framed glass. Brisk assistants, in natty uniforms, were folding the screen that had covered her mysterious passage through the solid crystal. Norgil, the magician, bowed to the applause that billowed in from the audience.

He was a superb showman, Norgil; suave to the tips of the pointed mustache that adorned his sophisticated, oval-chinned face. His wealth of jet-black hair showed at best as he took another bow. He displayed the ease of a dancing master when he sent the girl on a pirouette toward the wings.

Norgil followed, bowing himself off the stage. New notes from the orchestra crept into the applause. Hand claps finished as ears were haunted by the strains of spooky music. That melody was the prelude to Norgil's next mystery, his famous spirit cabinet.

In the wings, Norgil stopped by a large trunk where a

uniformed assistant was peeling off his monkey suit. Norgil soft-toned:

"All set for it, Fritz?"

Fritz raised his head. Norgil saw his face in the backstage light. He gave an approving nod; moved swiftly away. Fritz remained beside the trunk, finishing his preparation for a coming task.

The glass penetration had been performed "in one"— in theatrical parlance, before a curtain styled a "front drop." The spirit act called for a full-stage set; and the lights were dimming as the curtain slicked upward on its wires. A hush had gripped the audience; the darkened theater was stilled throughout.

Norgil felt that silence. It always came before the spirit cabinet trick. Music lulled until its weird strains were scarcely audible. These were the moments that brought the spectators to the edges of their chairs. On the bare stage they saw a skeleton cabinet, its chromium posts and crossbars reflecting the subdued light.

There was a floor to that cabinet. It was thin, and raised above the stage. There were curtains hanging at the corners; but their sheen showed that they were too thin to hide concealed assistants. The only object in the cabinet was a chair, where Norgil was to seat himself.

Yet, once the magician drew those curtains, ghosts would materialize within the cabinet. Norgil never claimed his spooks to be real, but there were credulous persons who considered them as such. Even doubters became tense when the spirit act was on. The trick was Norgil's masterpiece.

THERE was a figure coming on the stage. It was Norgil. His steps were dramatic in their slowness. He reached the cabinet; closed every curtain except the front one. The audience saw Norgil seat himself. His face was solemn, almost mystic. Like a man in a trance, he stretched his hand; he drew the front curtain shut.

Music had ceased. A dozen seconds passed, while tense viewers waited for weird, glowing faces to press aside the curtains. There were whispers in the audience, mild gasps of strained expectancy. Most of those sounds were lost. There was one, however, loud enough for some to hear.

That was a hissing sigh that came from a lower box. Timed to that odd tone, the curtain of the cabinet quivered. That motion held the audience. Their eyes fixed toward the stage, those who had heard the sigh forgot it.

Only an expert could have identified that sound and linked it with the curtain's stir. The sigh wasn't a human one, nor a ghostly manifestation. It was the suppressed hiss of a rifle equipped with a silencer. The motion of the cabinet's curtain marked the winging passage of a bullet, aimed straight for the heart of the hidden magician.

That lone shot fired, the marksman slid to the side aisle, packing his portable rifle beneath his coat. He wanted to get out of the theater before people wondered why the act didn't continue. From the darkness of the aisle, the satisfied murderer looked over his shoulder. He noted the gloomy cabinet, its front curtain motionless.

An instant later, the scene changed. The orchestra, taking a special cue, shrieked lively music. The stage flooded with light. Assistants bounded from the wings, whipped the curtains from the skeleton cabinet.

It was empty, except for the chair. Norgil was gone. He had changed his spook routine into a vanishing act.

Before the foiled marksman moved a step, he was treated to a second surprise, which he alone of all the audience could appreciate. Crouched in the darkness of the aisle, the gunner felt rounded steel freeze his neck.

With the revolver muzzle came the undertone:

"I'll take that toy. Turn around; keep moving, with your hands high."

The captured crook was thrust through a passage leading from the aisle, past the boxes. A fireproof door slid open; the unsuccessful killer was backstage. The revolver muzzle prodded him toward a dressing room, where a half-opened door bore a star. Stumbling down the steps, the surly prisoner turned about at a new command.

His captor was Norgil!

Norgil had handed the portable gun to Fritz, who was now beside him. As Norgil lowered his revolver, the crook sprang up the steps, only to meet a swift uppercut from Norgil's free fist. Sprawling back downward in the dressing room, the crook lay stunned while Norgil told Fritz: "Watch him while I work the first act. We'll quiz him later."

Five seconds later, Norgil was using the revolver with which he had cowed the would-be murderer. He was firing it at a tub of water, from which dripping ducks appeared in quick succession, flopping to the stage in accompaniment to the blank shots from the magician's gun.

Fritz made a bad mistake during the duck act. He left the unconscious prisoner to stow the fellow's gun in a trunk. While there, Fritz changed to his uniform. When he came back to the dressing room, the lights were out. Before Fritz could click the switch, the crook piled upon him.

He was tough, that crook. His quick recovery from Norgil's punch proved it, and Fritz couldn't pack the wallop that Norgil could. That fight in the dark produced a quick result. The prisoner slung Fritz across the dressing room; the assistant did a sprawl beside the wall.

Fritz rallied, too late. The door slammed; a key turned in the outside lock. By the time Fritz's pounding brought a stagehand to unlock him, the prisoner was gone. He had ducked out through the stage door, gunless, but free.

Norgil learned that when the show was over. Seated in his dressing room, the magician took pad and pencil. He produced a portrait, as accurate as it was speedy.

"Remember the lightning sketches I used to do at Coney?" asked Norgil. "Years ago, Fritz, but I haven't lost the touch. There's the ape who tried to wing you. Find out who he is."

Fritz left with the ex-prisoner's picture. Norgil smeared his face with cold cream; toweled away his makeup. Someone rapped at the door. Norgil tied the sash of his dressing gown and called for the visitor to enter.

It was Rickenbury, the theater owner; a big, bulldozing man, whose tuxedo was as paunchy as his jowlish cheeks. Rickenbury had a squawk to make. He delivered it in booming tone.

"What went sour with the spook stuff, Norgil? That vanish wasn't in your regular act."

"I know it." Norgil eyed the theater owner in the dressing table mirror. "Sometimes I make changes. No reason for you to object. I've bought the house."

Rickenbury's boom dwindled to a grumble. A wince came with it. Rickenbury had made a bad bet, leasing the theater outright to Norgil for two thousand dollars. He was wishing that he had played the magician on a percentage, instead. Business had been building every day; Norgil was likely to gross eight thousand for the week.

"Mayor Davison was here," explained Rickenbury. "He wanted to see the spook show. You disappointed him. Joland Frew was in the house, too. You know how important he is?"

Norgil nodded. Joland Frew was the biggest real estate promoter in the city. Public rumor rippled that Frew owned half the town.

"They'd like to meet you, Norgil—"

"All right, Rickenbury." Norgil came to his feet. "Show them in."

Mayor Davison proved a withery old fossil. His handshake was crablike; his laugh a cackle. Frew was middle-aged, square-built and genial. He didn't have much to say, for Mayor Davison took the floor.

"I wanted to see a ghost," cackled the mayor. "But there wasn't any. Why not, Mr. Norgil?"

Norgil gave a nonchalant smile. If he had gone through with his usual cabinet act, there *would* have been a ghost: his own. He didn't tell that to the mayor. Instead, Norgil simply replied:

"I wasn't in a psychic mood."

His honor didn't know how to take that explanation. He fancied that Norgil was jesting, but wasn't sure. Norgil's face sobered; he picked a sheet of paper from an inside pocket of his dress suit.

"This worried me," admitted Norgil. "Tell me what you make of it, Mr. Mayor."

The paper was a printed billhead that bore the title: "Theatrical Protective Association." It called for payment of twelve hundred dollars. The bill was made out to Norgil. At the bottom was the typewritten reminder: "Overdue. Remit before 10 p.m."

Mayor Davison showed a rankled expression. The city was in the grip of a racket ring that took its toll from many businesses. The mayor had promised to curb that crookery. But he hadn't. In fact, the cogwheels of the racket game had spun even more merrily since Davison had taken office.

To cover his embarrassment, his honor turned to Rickenbury. Plaintively, the mayor announced:

"This is a new one on me, Rickenbury. Have you known about it?"

The theater owner gave a reluctant nod.

"Why didn't you report it?"

"What was the use?" grumbled Rickenbury. "That outfit's

NORGIL—MAGICIAN 25

got me stopped. They call for fifteen percent on what they think the house is going to gross. I've paid it, to avoid trouble. This week, Norgil bought the house; so they passed the buck to him."

"Who are they?"

Rickenbury shrugged. He didn't know; apparently, he wasn't anxious to find out. The mayor questioned Norgil.

"I've been getting phone calls," stated the magician. "Always some fellow with a faked voice. Always the same argument: if I'm ready to pay up, he'll tell me how. A stage-hand answered the last of those calls at quarter of ten tonight, just before I went on with the penetration illusion. I said I couldn't be bothered."

Frew was studying the billhead. In caustic tone, the promoter expressed his indignation. Some of his own enterprises had been hit by the racketeers, but they hadn't yet come after him in a big way. Frew was beginning to think it wouldn't be long before they did. He was therefore interested in Norgil's case. Frew asked the magician what he intended to do about it.

"I'm carrying twelve hundred here," replied Norgil, spreading his dressing gown to show a money belt, "just in case they want the money bad enough to come after it. Otherwise, I don't pay up."

THE listeners liked Norgil's stand. Mayor Davison, in particular, approved it, especially when his honor saw a chance to change the touchy subject. The mayor suggested that they have some drinks and a midnight supper at the club. Norgil accepted the invitation, then remembered something.

"I'll meet you later," he said, as he donned his street clothes. "I have to take Daphne over to the hotel first." His tie adjusted, Norgil opened the door and called: "Fritz! Bring Daphne!"

Mayor Davison tilted his head and gave a withery smile. He was anxious to see which one of the pretty girls Daphne was. There were plenty of good-lookers in Norgil's troupe; probably Daphne was the damsel who had walked through the plate glass. His honor was hoping that she would arrive in the same scanty costume that she had worn during that illusion.

The mayor's face drooped when Fritz arrived and handed Daphne to Norgil. Daphne was a wire-haired fox terrier, scarcely more than a pup. Norgil was amused by the mayor's change of expression. So was Frew, who also noted it.

Once outside the stage door, Norgil bundled Daphne under his dark overcoat. His long, easy paces took him swiftly from the alley. He darted quick, expert looks as he crossed the back street. He was sure that no one was watching him. The same was true all along the back route to the hotel. Norgil was unobserved when he entered a sheltered rear doorway, to take a little-used stairway to the third floor.

Corridors were empty. Norgil's room was unwatched. The magician wore his suave smile as he neatly unlocked the room door. Inside the room, Norgil purred to Daphne:

"We're going to stay in the dark a while. You're used to it, pup, since I've been putting you in that place where you can't chew shoes. We won't have long to wait, though."

Chapter II
THE RIGHT HUNCH

NORGIL EXPECTED strategy with the coming thrust. There might be a bluff to throw him off his guard. If such came, it would only prove a boomerang to those who tried it. Bluff was part of Norgil's own technique; he could recognize it.

He was fooled, though.

The telephone bell jangled. Norgil suppressed the summons almost instantly. The telephone was on a table right beside him. As he gripped it, he lifted the receiver from the hook.

That ring could be a signal for someone who had sneaked into the third-floor corridor. That was why Norgil's mind was intent on the door, while his lips purred a "hello" into the telephone's mouthpiece.

The voice that answered made Norgil forget the door. It was Fritz, giving eager news. Fritz had shown Norgil's sketch to a friendly cashier in an all-night hash house. He had identified the ugly face as belonging to "Toughey" Eward, one of the town's reputed gunmen.

"A local cowboy," mused Norgil, voicing his thoughts softly across the wire. "Good work, Fritz. Find out some more about him. I still want to talk to him."

Norgil's own tone was to cause him trouble. It prevented him from hearing the turn of the door handle. Norgil had left the door unlocked; he was counting on hearing it if it opened. He was depending, too, on the corridor lights. But they had been extinguished.

Norgil hung up the receiver. Before he could sense that someone had entered the room, the arrival announced himself. There was the snap of a light switch by the door. Norgil bounded from his chair, too late. The room was filled with light from ceiling sockets. He was covered by a steady revolver, gripped by a hand below a bandana-masked face.

The stocky, ill-dressed intruder meant business. He wasn't a sneaky marksman like Toughey Eward. The fellow had the way of a professional stickup artist. He nudged Norgil toward a corner; then showed a long chin, as he growled:

"I'm here to get that dough, lug. Peel off that money belt— an' go easy when you do it. None of that sleight-o'-hand baloney."

Norgil kept his right hand raised, while he dipped his left fingers to the bottom of his vest, where the clasp of the money belt was. The masked crook watched those fingers closely, particularly one that wore a two-headed snake ring, gold with jeweled eyes.

Norgil made his move openly, carefully. He could guess that the crook's revolver had a hair trigger. The fellow had him, hands down, thanks to Fritz's ill-timed phone call. Luck had put Norgil on the spot. He didn't like it. Not because of the twelve hundred dollars that he was going to lose, but on account of the stupid way he had to hand it over.

Norgil would have paid twice the twelve hundred for a way out of this dilemma. Suddenly, he saw one. It was his turn for a lucky gift, but he needed nerve to back it.

What Norgil saw was a quiver of a closet door, only five feet from the masked thug's left shoulder. Norgil happened to know the symptoms of that door. It trembled again; another shake like that, and it would be loose. The thought steeled the magician.

Norgil let his left hand come up like his right. That brought a savage threat from the masked crook; with it, a gun nudge.

"Hey, you—don't try no stall——"

"There's no stall about it," interposed Norgil. "You're hooked, fellow, that's all. You were a sap to walk into it."

The crook's eyes glared doubt through the slits of the bandana. He didn't like the shrewd smile that Norgil seemed trying to restrain.

"The house dick's got you covered," added Norgil. "That's why I brought him up here. I had a hunch you'd be due, because——"

Norgil did not complete the reason. There was no need for it. The closet door had started a swing, although the masked gunman didn't hear its groan. Turning his head toward the door, Norgil kept on talking. That, likewise, was something the crook didn't guess. Norgil's lips had fixed. His words were a deep-throated tone; gruff, delivered in a ventriloquist's pitch:

"I gotcha, guy! Hoist those dukes. Hurry it!"

No lip motion was needed in any of those syllables. The illusion was perfect. Though close to Norgil, the armed crook would have sworn that the words came from the closet. Wheeling, the rowdy saw the closet door swinging outward.

Norgil was right about the hair trigger. The crook pumped bullets into the darkened closet, aiming on a level of a man's chest. He thought he had beaten the imaginary house dick to the shots. He remembered Norgil, but that came too late.

THE magician charged. His left hand nabbed the crook's gun. His right drove a hard uppercut. The crook's lucky twist saved him from that punch. As the gun went flinging across the room, the masked man came to grips.

As they thrashed the floor, they had a witness. It was Daphne. The pup came loping from the closet. Daphne had shoved that door loose once before, when Norgil had stowed her in the closet. Norgil had remembered it when he saw the door tremble. He'd taken a long chance that it would swing loose, as it had before. Chances, though, belonged to the stage magician's game. Guessing when to take them was something that Norgil had learned through long experience. He had outwitted entire audiences when he played long odds. Here, he had needed only to fool one man.

Norgil was using more headwork against the grappling crook. The fellow gained an advantage. Norgil's quick hand offset it. He couldn't grab the crook's throat; instead, he snatched the bandana mask and pulled it sideways. The eye slits slid to the crook's ear. The bandana became a blindfold.

By the time the oath-fuming crook had snatched off the improvised mask, it was Norgil who had the edge. He held the crook's neck; was ready to batter the man's head against the wall, when the hall door opened to show the startled face of a house detective.

Norgil did a sudden, backward sprawl. The elated crook lunged down upon him, only to receive Norgil's feet against his chest. With propelling power, Norgil catapulted the crook across the floor. His wind knocked out, the man slumped panting at the house dick's feet.

That finished matters. Together, Norgil and the house detective marched the gasping thug downstairs and turned him over to the police. Norgil left the hotel to have his midnight supper at the Town Club. Once there, he asked for Mayor Davison. An attendant showed him to a reserved table.

ONLY Joland Frew was there. Rickenbury had been detained at the theater; Mayor Davison had stopped off at the city hall. Frew had obligingly come ahead. While Frew was mentioning that, Mayor Davison arrived. Rickenbury showed up a few minutes later.

All became tense listeners when they heard Norgil's account of the hotel episode. The mayor promised speedy justice to the crook who had been captured. Frew congratulated Norgil on the effective way he had saved his twelve hundred dollars. Rickenbury expressed the hope that this would make the racketeers lay off theaters in the future; but didn't speak as though he counted on it.

Not one of the trio mentioned the idea that was paramount in Norgil's mind. They didn't seem to recall that they, alone, had known that the magician intended to return to the hotel. It was plain to Norgil, though, that the masked collector who had visited him had come at a tip-off from one of these three.

Perhaps the big shot was ready to drop the matter. Norgil

would be gone next week. The prestige of the racket ring could be restored without the collection of the magician's twelve hundred dollars—paltry change, compared to all that the big shot had at stake.

But Norgil wasn't ready to forget the racketeer. By tomorrow, if need be, he'd have new bait—the sort that any fish would swallow. His companions were discussing a special show, scheduled for tomorrow midnight. It was a convention affair, in the ballroom of the local hotel. They wanted Norgil as a headliner on the bill.

Obligingly, the magician agreed; but his smile meant more than ordinary willingness. Norgil was picturing how neatly that event could top off his plan to wreck the racket ring.

Chapter III
CASH DELIVERED

NEXT DAY, Fritz termed the matinee a "flopperoo"; and Fritz was right. Norgil wasn't himself on stage. He showed it when he fumbled the fish bowls; again, when he opened the door too soon with the Upside-Down Cabinet. The audience would have caught that one, if Fritz hadn't faked a stumble against the door to bounce it shut.

When Norgil wasn't right, the rest of the company felt it, too. The show ended with weak applause from the audience. On the way to their dressing rooms, the assistants muttered that the wizard had the jitters. That pleased Norgil, when he overheard it. If he could fool his own company with fake nervousness, he could put it across on others.

Norgil was at dinner when a bellhop called him to the telephone. A forced voice repeated the old question: was he ready to pay up? Norgil replied in the affirmative. The voice growled instructions.

"Stick the dough in an envelope. Put it in a coat pocket and send your suit down to the tailor shop. Before eight o'clock. That's all."

Soon after dinner, Fritz found Norgil in his hotel room. The magician was pacing the floor, smoking his fifth cigarette, while Daphne chewed slippers unmolested. Norgil told the assistant what was up, then motioned toward the open closet. A suit was hanging there. Norgil ordered Fritz to take it to the tailor shop.

That brought a flash of Fritz's pluck.

"Not a chance, boss," he argued. "Say, I did the double in the spook cabinet, didn't I? You don't think I'd have gone through with that, if I'd known that you were quitting cold—"

Norgil's hand thwack interrupted. It was planted on the middle of Fritz's back.

"Good boy, Fritz." It was the steely tone that the assistant had expected. "I knew you'd be ready for another stab at it. I wouldn't be sending the money along, if I didn't like the setup. I've looked into it, though, and I like it."

Norgil penciled a diagram. It showed a pair of long, narrow connecting rooms, with only one door at the front.

"The tailor shop," he explained. "In the basement. No windows. Only this door. What goes in there, comes out there."

Fritz nodded. He could see advantages in that.

"We've broken in that new man," recalled Norgil. "He can take your place, Fritz. You won't be needed at the theater. You'll be needed right over here."

Emphatically, Norgil dotted a diagram to indicate a spot across the street from the tailor shop, where Fritz was to watch. He added the remark:

"Whoever carries that money out will take it to the big shot. We'll risk the cash, Fritz, on the chance of a trail."

The evening show was finished earlier than usual, for Norgil sped up the program. He found Fritz at the watch-post; and the assistant had glum news. There had been a rush of business at the tailor shop. Half a dozen bellboys had come and gone on frequent visits. Each had carried away an average of five suits, all tuxedoes.

"It's the convention," explained Fritz. "And those bellhops were delivering pressed suits to rooms, instead of to people. There's thirty suits to pick from, all alike. It's a cinch the money went with one of them—"

"No one else entered the shop?"

"Nobody. There was a kid stopped and handed in a kettle of coffee to the old tailor. But the old guy didn't pass anything out. He's still in there, the tailor. Been busy as a monkey, I guess, though most of those suits were pressed earlier."

"Nobody except the tailor."

Norgil's purred interjection snapped Fritz to new life. Fritz had been thinking of the bellboys, not of the tailor. It struck Fritz suddenly that the magician had expected this very result. That was why he had gambled on it. While Fritz was still bubbling his admiration of Norgil's foresight, the magician drew him across the street.

It didn't take long for Norgil to finish the lock on the shop door while Fritz kept watch. The light in the front room was out. Norgil edged through the door and beckoned Fritz to follow. The rear part of the shop was lighted. That was where the tailor did his mending and handled the pressing machine.

The tailor was there. Fritz grinned as he saw the fellow resting with arm and head upon the mending table, sound asleep. Needles, thread and a patch of black silk lining lay beside the man's half-finished cup of coffee. He'd be due for a sudden surprise, that tailor, when Norgil woke him up.

There, Fritz guessed wrong. The surprise was to be his own. It was Norgil who suspected the real situation. The magician placed his hands upon the sides of the tailor's head and tilted the man's face upward. He looked into bulgy, sightless eyes. The head had inert weight when Norgil let it drop.

A tool of the racket ring, the tailor had been no longer needed. He was one man who had learned too much. That problem had been settled—by a delivery of poisoned coffee. The tailor was dead.

Chapter IV
BLADES OF STEEL

NORGIL RECALLED what Fritz had said about the parade of bellboys to and from the tailor shop. That procession had been part of the big shot's game. It broke the trail, as Fritz had supposed; and it ruined Norgil's bet, since the tailor was dead.

Rickenbury—Davison—Frew. All would be at the hotel tonight. Each would be dressing in tuxedo. By this time, the big shot—whichever he was—had collected the listed money.

What would he do with it?

"Come along, Fritz." Norgil's tone was low. "We're going to talk with a taxi driver about a rat."

They found the right taxi in front of the hotel, where people were already arriving for the convention show. Norgil questioned the fellow about Toughey. The cabby had never heard of him.

The man was lying, but that couldn't be helped. Norgil sized him as a small-fry hoodlum in the racket ring's employ. Even a gun threat wouldn't make him tell where Toughey was. If the taxi driver spilled what he knew, he'd get bullets from his own pals later.

Fritz didn't catch that point. He was reaching for the cab door when Norgil stopped him with a shin kick that the driver didn't see.

"Come along, Fritz," voiced the magician, smoothly. "We don't have to waste time with this bird."

That remark brought a quick look from the cabby. It seemed to have significance that applied to Toughey Eward. The cabby strained his ears as Norgil drew Fritz back from the curb. Norgil spotted the cab driver's interest, and used it.

The magician could use a stage whisper to perfection. He had a *sotto voce* tone that carried every word, although it seemed to be deliberately hushed. The cabby never guessed that Norgil's whisper was intended for his benefit.

"That note the tailor left," undertoned Norgil, intervening to hide Fritz's puzzled blink from the cabby. "It named the big shot. That's all we need. Let's go to the theater and get the affidavit from the dressing room."

Fritz managed a nod. He turned in the direction of the theater. Norgil stopped him with a smile. He nudged toward the hotel coffee shop; remarked, in a normal tone:

"There's time for a cup of coffee first."

They'd hardly passed the revolving door before the taxi whipped away. Its driver was off with an urgent message for Toughey. Fritz expected Norgil to grab another cab and follow. Instead, the magician insisted on his coffee. Fritz ordered milk. Coffee didn't interest him, after that visit to the tailor shop.

Five minutes later, they headed for the theater. Stage hands were through with their work, but the stage door wasn't locked. Cleaners would attend to that when they were through out front. Norgil turned on a light. The stage showed dim, with the big asbestos curtain as a barrier between it and the house.

Norgil stopped Fritz before they reached the dressing

room steps. They were beside the sword box, a squarish
cabinet mounted on high legs. Its heavy sides and door had
slits through which the swords could be thrust. The blades,
big cavalry sabers, were arranged in orderly fashion upon a
rack beside the wall.

There was an oddity about the sword box tonight. Usually,
it was turned with its door toward the stage. At present, it
had been shifted so the hinged door faced the dressing room.
Norgil observed that, but Fritz didn't. That was why the
magician, alone, saw the slight motion of the door.

Norgil didn't go past the front of the box. Instead, he
pressed one hand to his lips; motioned with the other for
Fritz to hand him a sword. Fritz was perplexed, but he
obeyed, with the absolute silence that Norgil wanted. Receiving the saber, Norgil gestured for Fritz to take one,
also. The assistant obliged.

Pointing his sword at one angle, then the opposite, Norgil
indicated that they were to deliver similar thrusts. His nod
was the final cue. Norgil shoved his sword through a side hole
in the box. The point came stabbing out through the front.
Simultaneously, Fritz's blade thrust into sight. The sword
points almost clicked.

THERE was a scuffle in the box as an occupant tried to
open the door. He failed; the swords had locked it. Norgil
grabbed another saber, started it through the side, crosswise
near the front. There was a howl; a body floundered backward to avoid the poke of the sword.

With a few swords still remaining on the rack, Norgil and
Fritz could find no further paths for them. The magician
mounted the platform, lifted off the box lid and handed it
to Fritz. The assistant peered over from the other side.

In the box, they saw a panting prisoner, in the person of
Toughey Eward. The thug had a gun, but he could neither

reach it nor use it. He'd dropped the revolver when he dodged a sword. Steel blades, thrust from varying angles, had contorted Toughey's scramble. He was twisted askew; his body was girded with the crossing sabers. So were his arms and legs. The sharp blades had them hunched in different directions.

"Keep him that way, Fritz," ordered Norgil. "If he gets too nervous, warm up some of the coffee we brought from the tailor shop. Toughey might like a drink of it."

With that last thrust, Norgil stepped from the platform. Fritz and the steel-bound prisoner heard the stage door slam as the suave magician departed to settle his final score.

Chapter V
BETTER THAN RABBITS

NORGIL WAS the sparkling attraction of the midnight show at the hotel. Most of the audience had seen his stage performances; they were treated to a different Norgil, whose close work held them awed. Cards materialized at the tips of long, deft fingers; coins vanished with a similar ease.

All the while, the magician's suave smile seemed to say that greater surprises were to come. His well-chosen program showed that design. Spectators wondered if each new trick could match the one before it. Norgil never disappointed them. He was building to a climax that this audience wouldn't forget.

In various tricks, Norgil required the assistance of the audience. He remarked that his final experiment needed the help of three spectators—prominent persons well known to every one present. He didn't have to suggest the names. People called them.

Mayor Davison was one; Joland Frew another. Norgil was inviting them to the platform, while the audience wrangled about who was to be the third. Norgil's tapering hand raised, to quiet the unsettled clamor. Since there was doubt, he would choose the third man to aid him. Norgil picked Rickenbury.

His final effect, Norgil announced, was an improvement over an older mystery. Undoubtedly, members of the audience had seen the famous Hindu Needle Trick, which had often been presented by Houdini. Norgil's version required other implements than needle and thread.

To the mayor, Norgil gave a glass of water. He handed Frew a length of fish line. For Rickenbury, he opened a package of double-edged razor blades, asking that they be examined. Rickenbury made the inspection, gingerly.

Taking the fish line from Frew, the magician coiled it into a compact wad, placed this on his tongue. He took a swallow from the glass of water. When he opened his mouth, the fish line was gone. Norgil reached for the razor blades.

There were gasps from the audience as Norgil's fingers carefully set the blades, one by one, upon his outstretched tongue. A back tilt of his head, and Norgil finished the glass of water. Amazed eyes watched the swallow that he made. Norgil grimaced as he shook his black-haired head. Coolly, he opened his mouth wide.

The razor blades had followed the fish line.

NORGIL'S smile met the startled gaze of those about him. The magician was thinking of other blades of steel—those swords that still encased Toughey Eward. That thought was scarcely more than a flash. Norgil's mind returned to the trick that he was now performing.

He reached to his lips; drew forth a razor blade, with easy, but careful motion. Attached to the blade was the end of the fish line. As it paid out, Norgil reached with his fingers to slide another blade from between his lips. The rest were following, a full dozen of them, while the first blades dangled. With the last, Norgil stretched his hands apart. There was the entire line of razor blades, knotted at regular intervals.

Applause was terrific. Nonchalantly, Norgil let his helpers examine the threaded blades. Obligingly, he sliced the fish line with the edge of a blade, so that each man could inspect a different segment of the cord. An odd blade remained in Norgil's right hand. As he turned to lay it on a table, his left thumb turned the snake ring that was on the third finger.

Instead of putting the loose razor blade aside, Norgil let his right thumb jab the end between the two heads of the snake ring. The blade pressed tight in place, flat against the palm of Norgil's left hand. Neither edge quite touched his flesh.

Mayor Davison was stepping from the platform. Norgil stopped him with a right-hand gesture. Reaching to his own coat pocket, the magician produced a timepiece that dangled on its chain.

"Your watch, your honor."

The audience roared its laughter as the stupefied mayor received the watch. From that same right pocket, Norgil brought a flat wallet that he tendered to Rickenbury, with the quizzical comment:

"Yours?"

Rickenbury nodded, while the laughter increased. Frew, in the center of the platform, was indulgently feeling his own pockets. He shook his head to indicate that nothing was missing. Norgil approached him.

"There's something under your coat collar, Frew——"

"A rabbit?" Frew laughed, as he raised his arms to the back of his coat. "I don't think so, Norgil. But maybe you can find one."

They were close together. Norgil was working swiftly, smoothly. Frew felt something beneath his coat, at the back. Norgil wanted him to notice it, so he would miss something else. The magician's left hand was busy, unseen by Frew and the audience. They were watching Norgil's right, as it came from the back of Frew's collar, bringing a string of silk handkerchiefs in front of the promoter's eyes.

Frew laughed; his mirth became hearty as Norgil followed with a line of baby's clothes. With another dip, he produced a whole fistful of silks that he clutched in his right hand. His left hand lowered. Its thumb flipped the razor blade loose, to fall noiselessly on the carpeted platform.

"Very good, Norgil," laughed Frew. "Nevertheless, I'd like a rabbit."

"No rabbits." Norgil's tone had become methodical. His left hand brought an envelope from his own inside pocket. "Here, Rickenbury, you hold the affidavit. And you, Mr. Mayor—"

As Norgil looked toward the mayor, Frew did the same. The magician's left hand darted with whipped speed inside the front of Frew's coat. From the long slit that the razor blade had sliced in the lining, Norgil whipped a compact envelope that crinkled from the currency inside it.

"Hold the money, Mr. Mayor," added Norgil. "The bills that match the numbers in the affidavit. Meanwhile, let me present"—he was on Frew's right, gesturing his left hand toward the promoter—"the big shot of this city's racket ring!"

FREW'S face was maddened. His clenched fists shook toward Norgil.

"A lie!" Frew's voice was a bellow. "You planted those on me, Norgil—"

"Hardly," purred Norgil. "I had to slice the lining of your coat to get the envelope."

"It wasn't in the lining—"

"Not until the tailor sewed it there. He was murdered neatly, Frew; but he left the black silk on his mending table."

That impeachment was enough for Frew. With murderous glare, the big shot sped his hand to his hip pocket. Spectators sprang for the platform, to grab him before he could pull his gun. They were too late to halt Frew's move. In his turn, Frew was tardy in seeking the revolver.

Norgil's right hand gave a flourish. The cluster of silk handkerchiefs scattered, drifted to the platform. In Norgil's fist was a pearl-handled .32, its muzzle pointing straight for Joland Frew. The big shot recognized that weapon, as he heard Norgil's dry comment:

"Yours, I believe."

A dozen hands fell on Frew. Still bellowing an innocence that no one believed, the head of the racket ring was dragged from the platform. Norgil joined Davison and Rickenbury. He added Frew's revolver to the money and the affidavit that were already exhibits on the table.

"Better than rabbits," was Norgil's smiling comment. "By the way, Mr. Mayor, there's a prisoner at the theater who will clinch the case against Frew."

Later, after Toughey Eward had joined Joland Frew in the city jail, Norgil expressed a whimsical thought. He voiced it to the mayor and the theater owner while they sat with the magician at a table in the Town Club.

"Each year," recalled Norgil, "I give a free performance at the state penitentiary. When I see Frew there, I'll have his rabbit for him."

Ring of Death

Chapter I
THE RING

THE SPOTLIGHT WAS focused upon the steps that led from stage to audience. Norgil had taken a bow for his last trick; the suave smile on his mustached face betokened that another mystery was due.

Slowly, Norgil descended the "rundown," the spotlight creeping with him, step by step. Even the intense glow could not betray the weariness that Norgil's smile covered. This was the last show on a five-a-day schedule; a hard grind, even for the black-haired magician, whose energy seemed as inexhaustible as his wizardry.

With a gesture, Norgil cued the projection booth. The spotlight circled the front rows of the audience. Norgil was watching for the type of person he wanted.

A girl in an aisle seat leaned back suddenly. She had been reaching forward, touching the shoulder of a man in the row ahead. He was slouched in his seat, eyes tilted downward, avoiding the spotlight. The light was past him, when Norgil's

43

next cue halted it; but the girl was caught in the circle.

"I should like to borrow a ring," spoke Norgil, his tone encouraging in its melody. "A lady's ring"—he was in the aisle; his eyes met the girl's, as if at random—"ah, perhaps this young lady has one that she will lend?"

The girl's gaze was nervous. Norgil's smile became soothing, friendly. Her reaction did not surprise the magician. There was something sensitive about the brunette girl's well-molded features and tight-pursed lips.

Lending a ring would be the easiest way for her to end the ordeal. That was the idea that Norgil's smile conveyed; and the answer came swiftly. The girl raised her hands, extended a ring so immediately that it scarcely seemed to come from her finger.

The rich green of an emerald shone in the light, but its luster was almost banished by the sparkle of the diamond cluster that surrounded it. That glitter was not lost until Norgil reached the stage, where the accompanying spotlight faded. From the darkness, the audience watched tensely.

A dapper assistant came on stage, bringing a long pistol. Norgil tried to force the ring into the muzzle. It wouldn't go. He snapped his fingers. The assistant brought a hammer. The soft rhythm of the orchestra was punctuated by gasps from the audience, when Norgil pounded the ring into the gun.

The spotlight was back again, sweeping up past the proscenium arch as Norgil elevated the pistol. The light found its focus on the theater dome, where a gilded, miniature pagoda hung by chains. The pistol's report cracked. The pagoda opened; from it floated a tiny parachute, weighted by a gem-encrusted ring!

Norgil was down the steps, leaving the pistol with the assistant. He was gauging where the parachute would land. He could hear the anticipating buzz of the spectators. The flash of that ring left no doubt in their minds. It was the very one that Norgil had borrowed!

A bald-headed man, four seats in, was holding his pudgy hands upward to catch the parachute. Norgil saved him that trouble. With a long stretch, the magician nipped the parachute on the fly. The house lights came on as he detached the ring from the cords.

Turning, Norgil began a bow to the young lady who had tendered him the ring. His lips were ready to phrase the usual question, asking her to identify the ring as the one that he had borrowed. Four times today, Norgil had worded that request. This time he stifled it.

The girl in the end seat was gone!

SKILL represented but part of Norgil's ability. In addition to dexterity, he possessed showmanship. He was out of that dilemma before the audience had time to grasp its existence. A blank-faced woman was seated farther back along the aisle. Ignoring the empty seat, Norgil stepped in her direction.

"Your ring?" he purred. "The one you gave me?"

Norgil's nod was the slightest; but it brought a dumfounded response from the gawking woman that he had picked as a temporary stooge. She nodded, very definitely; reached wonderingly for the ring. Norgil's fingers performed a deft pass. While it was dawning on the woman that she had no claim upon the ring, she discovered that the bauble wasn't in her hands at all.

The audience, though, was satisfied that Norgil had returned the ring to the person from whom he had borrowed it. The magician was back on the stage; border lights were ablaze and the orchestra was blaring the strident music of the finale.

Five minutes later, Norgil was in his dressing room, studying the borrowed ring through a jeweler's glass. Norgil was a connoisseur of jewelry; while on tour, he frequently made purchases of gems. The emerald was a flawless specimen; the diamonds, though small, were excellent.

Norgil appraised that piece at two thousand dollars. Its value made him consider other facts.

The setting was old-fashioned; the ring was evidently some heirloom. There were not many persons in this small city who could own such jewelry. A local inquiry could settle one question rapidly—whether or not the ring belonged in town. That would be the first step toward learning the identity of the worried brunette who had fled in the darkened theater.

Norgil came from the dressing room. Members of the troupe were about ready to leave by the stage door, with the exception of Fritz, the dapper assistant who was Norgil's right-hand man. Fritz was at a rear corner of the stage, working on a new cabinet.

LIKE many of Norgil's stage illusions, the cabinet was a curious contrivance. It stood upon a raised platform, and the cabinet itself was six feet high. It was three feet wide; and its side walls were four feet deep.

Walls, back, and top were constructed of shiny steel. The contrast was the door. It was nothing more than a flimsy wooden frame, covered with a huge sheet of paper. When Fritz saw Norgil approach, he gave a grin. Swinging the flimsy door outward on its hinges, Fritz gestured toward the cabinet's interior.

"All set, boss," informed Fritz. "Fixed like you wanted it. Step inside and try it——"

Norgil's headshake was an interruption. Fritz saw that the magician was concerned with some other matter.

"Remember what happened with the parachute, Fritz?"

"Sure. The gal didn't wait to get the ring back. What

was it—some five-and-dime junk?"

"Take a look."

Fritz whistled when he held the ring. Norgil gestured for him to put it in his pocket.

"Go down and see James Tibbington," undertoned Norgil. "He's the local jeweler that the usher brought backstage this afternoon. I told him I might drop into his shop tonight and look over what he had to offer.

"Ask Tibbington if he's ever seen this ring before. Get all the dope you can on it. Leave the ring with him, if he's willing, but get a receipt for it. Then hop over to my hotel room. Either wait for me, or leave a message—where nobody will bother it."

Fritz hurried out through the stage door, along with the rest of the company. Humming to himself, Norgil stood alone, eying the steel cabinet with approval. He was swaying the paper-framed door back and forth, when he noted a hollow murmur that came from beyond the asbestos curtain.

The audience had left, yet there was commotion in the theater. Norgil went through the passageway that connected with the house. As he slid a fireproof barrier aside, he looked through the curtains of a box; saw the reason for the murmurs.

A cluster of ushers were gathered at a row of seats near the orchestra pit. With them was Bill Trummel, the theater manager, mopping his baldish forehead with a silk handkerchief. Norgil vaulted the box rail. Joining the throng, he saw the ushers lifting a slumped man from a seat.

"Dead, all right," said an usher, his tone awed. "His weight tells that, Mr. Trummel. It must have been his heart—"

Norgil's gaze was set; his suave lips tight. He remembered the dead man; he had seen the fellow, slouched in that very seat. It was the man whose shoulder the mystery girl had been tapping, at the moment when Norgil had interrupted with his request for the brunette to lend him a ring!

Chapter II
NORGIL PROVES VERSATILE

BACK IN his dressing room, Norgil changed rapidly to street clothes. He hadn't told Trummel about the ring; the theater manager had enough worry for the present. The body had been carried from the theater, and was on its way to a hospital. After it reached there, the real cause of death would be learned. Norgil could see trouble popping for Trummel.

Norgil wanted to be gone before the police called at the dressing room. This would not cause complication. They would find him at the hotel, in an hour or so, after he came in from his usual midnight lunch. But Norgil did not intend to spend that interval at a restaurant. He was planning to follow the trail of the emerald ring; to find the girl at the end of it.

The magician was reaching for his hat, when a knock sounded at the dressing room door. Though Norgil's lips lost their smile, his purred voice was as smooth as ever.

"Who is it?"

"Clabby," came the reply. "A gent here wants to see you, Mr. Norgil."

Clabby was the long-faced usher who always conducted visitors backstage. Norgil told him to admit the caller. The door opened. Clabby was there, in his tight-fitting uniform; he stepped aside so that a bulky, derby-hatted man could pass. The fellow removed a cigar stump from his lips; gave a momentary flash of a badge beneath his coat, just as Norgil motioned for Clabby to wait.

"I'm Detective Handlen," informed the bulky man. "From headquarters. There's something I want to ask you about, Mr. Norgil."

"You mean the trouble out front?" questioned the magician. Handlen shook his head.

"It's not that," he returned. "This is about a ring that a young lady handed to you. She didn't get it back."

"Because she didn't stay," Norgil told him. "She did a vanishing act of her own."

"She got embarrassed," explained Handlen, "and left the theater. Her guardian called headquarters, told us to get the ring back for her."

Norgil's head was shaking; slowly, but emphatically. Handlen thrust his chin close to the magician's.

"Want me to pinch you?" demanded the bulky man. "On a theft charge?"

Norgil clapped a hand on the fellow's shoulder, took another grip on Handlen's coat lapel.

Norgil stepped back. IIis eyes went to his left hand, which he was holding cupped at waist level. His fingers flashed an object into the light; the article was shield-shaped and nickel-plated.

"This tin badge of yours, Handlen," said Norgil, "it looked phony when you flashed it. What hock shop gypped you with this piece of junk?"

Handlen charged with a bellow. Norgil sidestepped, took the phony dick with a half nelson. Handlen twisted, threw his bulk sideways to shake the grip. That wasn't bothering Norgil; he was counting on Clabby. He could hear the wiry usher clattering in from the doorway.

Then came confusion.

Norgil was clipped from two directions. Before he could recover from Clabby's surprise attack, the traitorous usher had relieved Handlen. The back of Norgil's head thudded a big trunk as he hit the floor. He lay there, eyes shut, and the room swept in dizzying circles.

There had been murder in the audience. Why should these crooks refrain from dealing death backstage?

That thought kept sweeping Norgil's whirling brain. It accounted for the part he played. To all appearances, that jolt against the trunk had knocked him cold. If his captors had decided to tap him on the skull, Norgil would have come to life, to put up a fresh battle. They decided, however, that it would be unnecessary to slug him; so Norgil continued his pretense.

The pair searched the magician in a hurry. Finding no trace of the ring, they began to scour the dressing room. On his side, Norgil watched Clabby with one open eye. He was planning a sudden surprise for the pair; but he held it too long. Handlen arrived before Norgil had a chance to spot him. The fake dick rolled Norgil on his face, began to bind his wrists in back of him.

Fight was doubly useless. Norgil was trapped; he knew, moreover, that the pair did not intend to kill him right away, for in that case the bonds would be useless. They plastered a chunk of adhesive across his mouth, hoisted him, and planked him into the big trunk. The lid slammed; Norgil heard a key turn. Clamps thumped into place.

There were muffled footsteps; the crooks were departing.

A thought struck Norgil—he could foresee disaster for others beside himself. Norgil wanted to make an escape in record time, but the confines of the trunk prevented it. The crooks had bound him with his own cords, the kind he particularly liked; but it was a long task, tightening those knots, to force slack into the ropes. At last Norgil's hands pulled free.

The trunk was stuffy. Norgil ripped the plaster from his lips, took long breaths of the stifling air. They'd figure this trunk would hold him, for it was heavily built, with special locks and big spring clamps. The sort of trunk that no one would crack in a hurry, from the outside.

Inside, it was different. Norgil broke open the big buckle of his belt. Stowed there was the tiny handle of a combination tool, with knife blade, awl, file and screwdriver. Using the tiny knife, Norgil slashed the lining of the trunk. He pulled the blade from the handle, inserted the screwdriver. They'd taken his fountain-pen flashlight, along with his matches; but Norgil managed without them.

He attacked the trunk hinges in the darkness. The inner screws came out. Short of oxygen, dizzy as he puffed the last vestiges of needed air, Norgil shouldered upward. The trunk lid gave; it opened at the back. Norgil shoved his head through the space and took five long breaths.

Chapter III
THE MISSING MESSAGE

BILL TRUMMEL was none too happy as he sat at his desk in the upstairs office. The theater manager was looking out at the lighted street, where the car had left, carrying the dead man to the hospital. The suspense was getting Trummel's nerve. He expected bad news.

The telephone bell rang. Trummel reached for the receiver. He heard a quick, wheezy voice behind him. He turned to see a stooped man, with thick mustache and Vandyke beard, who was carrying a small satchel. Trummel forgot the telephone for the moment.

"You're from the hospital, doctor?" questioned the theater manager. "Tell me—about the man we found here—"

The fingers of a kid glove hooked Trummel's elbow, none too gently. It was Norgil's voice that purred from the bearded lips:

"Come along, quick. I've got plenty to tell you. When we're outside."

"But the telephone—"

"Tell an usher to answer it. Say that you're leaving for the hospital."

They met an usher outside the office. The attendant hurried in to answer the telephone. They could hear his voice as they went down the stairs.

"What's that!" The usher was excited. "You say the man was poisoned. . . . But I can't tell Mr. Trummel to wait here. . . . He's already left. . . . Yes, for the hospital. . . . A doctor called for him. . . . Certainly, I'll try to overtake them."

Norgil and Trummel were already at the lower exit. They went left under the marquee, turned a corner before the usher saw them. On the way to the hotel, a few blocks distant, Norgil told Trummel exactly what had happened. The theater manager was amazed to learn of Clabby's treachery.

"We should have grabbed the fellow," began Trummel. "Maybe he's still at the theater—"

"He's gone with Handlen," interposed Norgil. "I took a good look, when I came up to your office."

"And they suppose, by this time, that you're dead. But what if they come back and find that empty trunk broken open?"

"They won't find it that way. I unlocked it with another key and fixed the hinges. It's locked again, with a big bag of sand inside to give it weight."

Ideas were drilling home to Trummel. The crooks had stowed Norgil away, alive, on the chance that they might want him later. For some reason, they had learned that wasn't necessary; so they had simply left him to die.

"They won't be back at the theater for nearly an hour," prophesied Norgil. "Clabby knows everything that is due there. Meanwhile"—they were at the door of the hotel— "we've got to learn what Fritz found out. Go to it, Bill."

TRUMMEL handled it capably. At the desk, he inquired casually for Norgil, as though he expected the magician to be in his room. After a short chat with the clerk, Trummel turned to the bewhiskered man who accompanied him, explaining:

"Mr. Norgil is still out to dinner. But his assistant, Fritz, came in a while ago. It will be all right for us to go up to the room and wait there, doctor."

The moment they entered the room, Norgil could tell what had happened. Fritz wasn't there, and it was plain that he had left under compulsion. Chairs, hastily reset, indicated that there had been a struggle.

Moreover, the place had been searched. Norgil's belongings were few; he kept most of his things at the theater. Bed pillows were rumpled; the rugs had been lifted. Even a few small tricks on a bureau had been moved about. Norgil told this to Trummel.

"They were after the ring!" exclaimed Trummel. "Do you think Fritz kept it?"

"I think they were after something more important," declared Norgil. "The message that Fritz was to leave for me."

"If he left one, they found it."

"I'm not so sure, Bill."

Norgil was applying cold cream to his face. It loosened the spirit gum that held his Vandyke. The makeup peeled away. Trummel noted the smile beneath Norgil's restored mustache.

"You haven't seen this trick, Bill." Norgil handed Trummel a pair of slates. "It's one I use when I give those midnight ghost shows. Take a good look at those slates."

"But this is no time for tricks," protested Trummel.
"It's time for this one." Norgil took the blank slates
from the theater manager. "Watch it closely."

NORGIL held the slates above his head. Trummel would
have sworn that he heard the scratch of an invisible slate
pencil; perhaps that was another of Norgil's clever methods.
The result, however, left Trummel flabbergasted.

Norgil separated the slates. Their surfaces bore writing,
in sharp chalk. Holding one slate in his left hand, the other
in his right, Norgil read from one, then continued with
the second slate.

"It's from Fritz," he declared. "I told him to leave a
message that nobody would find. He saw James Tibbington,
and left the ring with him."

"What else?" questioned Trummel. "Did Tibbington
know anything about the ring?"

"Yes. It's from the Dryden collection. Tibbington had
Fritz wait while he tried to call Mrs. Dryden; but couldn't
locate her."

"No wonder. Mrs. Dryden left for Europe this morning.
But she was supposed to have taken all her jewels with her.
It was understood that she intended to sell them abroad."

With that, Trummel outlined the history of the Dryden
jewels. They had been exhibited occasionally in past years.
After their owner's death, his widow had acquired them. With
heavy inheritance taxes, everyone had foreseen that she would
eventually turn the gems into cash. The total collection was
valued at more than one hundred thousand dollars.

"It begins to clear," declared Norgil. "Someone was
after those jewels, and managed to get them. That means
swindlers from out of town, putting up a big front, using
the girl in their game. There's just one place they'd use
as headquarters."

"This hotel?" asked Trummel.

"That's the answer," returned Norgil. "It's the only first-class hotel in town. Snagging Fritz was right down their alley. They've put him somewhere close at hand; our job is to learn where."

PICKING up the telephone, Norgil handed it to Trummel. He told Bill to call the desk; by the time Bill had lifted the receiver, Norgil was undertoning what he was to say.

Trummel inquired if a young lady had called to see Norgil. She—so Trummel stated—was seeking a job at the local theater. Norgil had recommended her; Trummel had come to interview her. Unfortunately, Norgil wasn't here; and Trummel didn't know the girl's name.

She was staying at the hotel, Trummel was sure of that. He could also describe her. Word for word, he repeated Norgil's whispered statements regarding the brunette's appearance. Trummel was eager when he hung up the receiver.

"She's here!" he told Norgil. "Her name is Miriam Laymond. She and her uncle, Richard Laymond, have Suite 610. There is another man, named Andreth, their chauffeur."

"Probably the fellow who called himself Handlen," observed Norgil. "Let's consider another matter. Tomorrow, my show packs up. But in about a half hour from now, some of the lighter luggage is going out ahead. Fritz was to be there when the trucks came. The stage door is unlocked."

Trummel nodded his recollection of the details.

"After you leave here," ordered Norgil, "call the truckers. You may find that they've been stalled off. Whether they have or not, get some trucks around in just about forty minutes. Have some of your local detectives in them."

"But if they're still itchy about that dead man——"

"They'll listen all the quicker, when you tell them you're out to bag the murderers."

Trummel went to the door. As he turned for a look toward Norgil, he saw the slates with their revealed message. Trummel muttered words that Norgil heard:

"It may have been a trick," voiced Trummel, "but it was like a message from the dead!"

Chapter IV
CROOKS TURN THE TIDE

THE INNER ROOM of Suite 610 was black, save for the patch where dim light trickled through the outer door. Through that opening bulked the big figure of Andreth, alias Handlen. He stopped where two figures lay bound and gagged, propped against the wall.

Andreth reached down and clutched a man's shoulder. The figure moved feebly. Andreth provided a hard kick that almost toppled the prisoner.

"Coming to, huh?" he grunted. "Better make the most of it. It won't be long before you get another sock on the konk, tougher than the one we handed you. Only the next time, you won't wake up."

The other prisoner stirred, tried to rise. Andreth stooped to deliver a contemptuous snarl. He saw the eyes of Miriam Laymond; met their flash of protest.

"We ain't croaking you," Andreth told the girl. "This guy gets shipped along with his boss—in another trunk. Only you're going out with us, just to keep up a front. A jab of dope in the arm, a gun poking you in the back— you won't raise a squawk.

"So you found some of the swag, huh? And guessed that Dick Laymond was a crook? Him, the guy you thought was your guardian; the fellow you called uncle. Only you pulled a dumb one, hopping over to the theater to find Terry Druke. You thought he was on the level, because he was the guy who introduced us to Mrs. Dryden.

"Only Terry was a crook, too. A wise guy, that figured he could double-cross us later. That's why we'd fixed it to croak him. But you didn't get nowhere, slipping the ring to Norgil. We tucked him in a safe place, and the same goes for the swag."

Andreth crossed the room, opened a window and looked downward. All was silent below; but the husky had orders to keep occasional watch from that window. There was a fire escape farther along the wall. It had been too close to suit Richard Laymond, head man of the visiting swindle workers.

Andreth closed the window. There was no use locking it; he was coming back soon for another look. He passed the prisoners, went into the lighted living room. After listening at the hallway door, Andreth flopped in a chair beside a floor lamp. He planked a gun on a table at his elbow, began to look through the pages of a pictorial magazine.

OUTSIDE the window of the inner room, Norgil was bridging the space between the fire escape and Andreth's lookout spot. Once he had located Suite 610, Norgil had seen the same possibilities that had occurred to Laymond.

Norgil, however, was acting in the capacity that the swindler had feared. Huddled on the fire escape, he had watched Andreth open and shut the window. The fellow's very vigilance was a weakness. With the window unlocked, Norgil had the sure route that he wanted.

Safely along a narrow cornice, Norgil worked the window sash upward. He edged over the sill, made out the forms of the prisoners. Peering toward the outer room, he guessed at Andreth's location, even though he couldn't see the fellow's corner. Norgil worked closer to the door.

From the right of the doorway, he saw a telephone, with a long extension cord; it was in the living room, on a table just to the left. He still could not spy Andreth; but the prisoners could. They saw Norgil, and they nodded. Norgil took a pace forward. Miriam began to shake her head, excitedly.

She had spotted something, before it dawned on Fritz. But it was too late for Norgil to halt his forward move. He had a gun in his right hand, but it was encumbered by the edge of the door. Letting the weapon sink into his pocket, Norgil changed tactics.

Through the doorway, he sped a swift look toward Andreth's corner. Grabbing the telephone, the magician darted back into the inner room.

Miriam's warning had not been groundless.

Andreth was coming up from his chair, grabbing the revolver as he slung the magazine aside. He saw Norgil snatch the phone; but the magician was away before the crook could aim. He was ducking to Andreth's left, out of sight in the inner room.

Three steps more were all Andreth needed to pass the doorway, where he could wheel to the left and riddle Norgil's corner with bullets. The crook took two of those long strides; the third finished him.

Something caught Andreth's shin, hooked the crook's foot and sent him headlong. As he sprawled, losing his revolver, Andreth saw Norgil standing with the telephone as his only weapon. The magician had drawn the cord tight, as Andreth charged. Stretched across the doorway, it formed an invisible obstacle in the gloom.

STILL clutching the telephone, Norgil reached Andreth as the fellow made a grab for his gun. This time the telephone served as a bludgeon, when Norgil swung it at Andreth's head. The crook took the blow behind the ear. He lay groggy while Norgil pocketed the fallen gun.

Norgil cut Fritz loose first, in case Andreth recuperated. Sitting on the slumped crook, Fritz told what he had heard Andreth say to Miriam. When the girl was freed, she corroborated the story, added other details.

"I can't understand how they acquired the gems," she told Norgil. "Andreth drove us out to see Mrs. Dryden, last night. My uncle said he wanted to buy the jewels—some of them for me—but he decided the price was too high.

"So we came back here without them. This morning, Mrs. Dryden left, taking the gems to Europe. Then, by accident, this evening, I found all of the jewelry here. I took one ring as evidence; but I couldn't spare much time.

"I was horrified when I saw Terry dead. I had to get back here before my uncle suspected. But he had learned, by the time I returned."

The girl paused, totally nonplussed.

"Clabby must have watched you," explained Norgil. "He was a crooked usher in the theater. As for last night, you've told me all I needed to know. Laymond unquestionably had a complete set of imitation jewels, representing the Dryden collection. He switched them out there, letting Mrs. Dryden keep the false gems."

Aided by Fritz, Norgil bound Andreth with suitcase straps that tightened like thongs. He gave Fritz his own gun; but kept the one that had belonged to Andreth. Drawing Fritz aside, he told him what came next.

"You'll hear from me in about fifteen minutes," he completed. "If matters are the way I think they are, you can go to the place that we know about. When you hear from me."

Miriam had an anxious query:

"Won't—won't my uncle be back here? With others—I know there are some—to help him?"

"He won't come here first," promised Norgil. "He has a preliminary job, where a reception committee will be waiting for him."

NORGIL left the suite by the fire escape. Shoulders slightly huddled, face well muffled, he made an inconspicuous figure as he detoured by a side street. Passing a dimly lighted arcade, Norgil entered an alleyway, stopped by a side door. There, he tried the lock, found it unlatched. That would do for Fritz when the time came.

Reaching the theater, Norgil sidled in by the stage door. Lights were on in the dressing room; the trunk was exactly as he had left it. Crossing the huge, dim stage, Norgil's footsteps were lost in the hollowness of that space.

From outside came the rumble of a solitary truck, stopping at the stage door. It was the one that Norgil expected first. He stepped to the backstage telephone, not far from the fireproof door that connected with the "house."

Dropping a nickel, Norgil called the hotel, asked for 610. Fritz answered; Norgil sped the low-voiced order:

"Get started. I'll join you there in ten minutes."

Hanging up, Norgil stepped away to avoid the glow of the nearest wall light. Men were entering from the stage door, far on the other side. They were too late to hear Norgil; nor could they see him. But there were others who did.

Norgil, himself, was aware of their arrival when the door from the house thumped shut automatically. From their angle, those entrants could spot him against the light. The first was Clabby, no longer in uniform; behind him was a tall, wince-faced man with gray hair, who wore evening clothes. Norgil knew that he must be Richard Laymond.

Both had guns. Drawing his own, Norgil sprang out toward the darkness of the stage. Clabby gave a hoarse yell, pulled a light switch. Four hoodlums, fake truckmen, stopped at the door of the dressing room, where they had gone to get the trunk. Those mobsters also whipped out guns!

Chapter V
CABINET OF DEATH

NERVE WAS NORGIL'S greatest asset. When he used it in the pinch, luck sometimes went with it. He knew he was trapped; his only course was to keep on the move, faster than those foemen could figure it.

They didn't expect him to head for that boxed corner of the stage; so that was where he went, with the tricky, shifty speed that accounted for his graceful poise in all his performances.

Crooks were closing in for close-range fire. Gun in hand, Norgil made another shift. They spotted his objective. It was the steel cabinet on which Fritz had completed work tonight. The paper door was wide open, showing its flimsy construction; but they could see the shine of the steel walls and the back.

Laymond bawled an order:

"Don't let him get behind that cabinet! He'll swing it with the back toward us! He'll get inside!"

Crooks spread to flank the cabinet. Their guns began to bark, waking long echoes from the fly loft and the gridiron, high above. Those bullets were ahead of Norgil, a barrage that zipped the space behind the cabinet to prevent him reaching there. It was Laymond who aimed point-blank at Norgil.

The magician swerved just before the swindler pulled the trigger. An instant later, he again performed the unexpected;

but this time, with a frantic fashion that suited a man maddened by terror.

Norgil did not pass the cabinet. Instead, he sprang inside it, boxing himself where crooks could get him. As if realizing the idiocy of his action, he made a move as ludicrous as that of a drowning man grasping the well-known straw.

Snatching a strap that hung from the paper-framed door, Norgil yanked the barrier shut. The action brought a raucous guffaw from Laymond. As the hoodlums semicircled up beside the swindler, Laymond rasped:

"Give it! Before he pokes out and starts to shoot."

SIX guns broke loose. Murderers found satisfaction in those shots. Their bullets peppered the paper frame; left holes that were testimony to the accuracy of the marksmen. Each killer wanted to better the efforts of the others. Like Laymond, they emptied their guns. The paper door was dotted from top to bottom, as proof that Norgil's body had been riddled.

"Drag him out!" snapped Laymond. "Pack him in that trunk. Get over to the hotel before the cops pile in here!"

Three crooks were piling forward to fight for the privilege of revealing Norgil's corpse, when the door opened of its own accord. Standing there, ready with his gun, was Norgil; his suave smile returned.

As a jest, perhaps, he had not troubled to cover the reason of his escape from the riddling fire.

From the center of each side wall extended half-opened flaps of steel. Actuated from the floor of the cabinet, those hidden obstructions had slammed shut the moment that Norgil passed them.

"My bullet-proof cabinet," purred Norgil. "It goes in the act next week. Working splendidly, isn't it? Foolproof, too. It will wow the audience when a girl steps in, and my assistants drill the front with rifles."

The crooks didn't try to raise their guns. And just then, there was a clatter from the stage door. Trummel had arrived with the detectives. They were piling in to make a roundup. Laymond's mob went mad, as they dove for the dicks with swinging guns.

Police revolvers stopped that surge. Slugging crooks went sprawling on the stage as bullets clipped them. There were shots, too, from the cabinet, from Norgil's revolver; but he was not downing the mob with a rear fire. Norgil was fighting off two men whose lives depended on his death. Laymond and Clabby were trying to slug him to the cabinet floor.

It was Clabby who took the bullets that Norgil was forced to fire. Wildly, the traitor clung to his foeman, trying to drag him down. Norgil's gun shoved for Laymond; but the swindler was away. He reached the fireproof door; was through it, when Norgil fired.

Barking shots above the slumped shoulders of Clabby, Norgil heard them wham the sliding barrier as it shut. Springing from the cabinet, Norgil followed, letting the police finish up the mob.

FOLLOWING Norgil's instructions, Fritz had reached the little alley where the magician had detoured on his way to the theater. Miriam was with Fritz; she was puzzled by this destination. Fritz opened the door and beckoned her through. There was a passage, then a door that Fritz whipped open.

A smallish man with white eyes and yellowed teeth came bobbing from a safe front. They were in a little office that looked like a jeweler's shop; across from them was an entrance, with frosted panel. The smallish man saw Fritz's gun, tried to duck into another room.

"No go, Tibbington." Fritz halted the fellow's flight

with those words. "Norgil's wise to your game—even though I wasn't. Fork over those Dryden gems."

Fumbling, Tibbington produced the jewel cases, let them fall open. Miriam recognized the whole collection. With the rest of the jewels was the ring that she had given Norgil.

"The boss had it figured right," spoke Fritz to Miriam. "It was Clabby who brought Tibbington backstage today, for a visit that didn't mean much. After Clabby showed himself phony, Norgil figured he was the go-between; that Tibbington had come to see him."

Fritz grinned tightly.

"It took a local crook to dig up those imitation gems that had been used for exhibitions. Tibbington supplied them to your uncle, so he could make the switch.

"There was something else that Norgil saw was phony" —Fritz spoke this straight to Tibbington—"that was your calling up to find if Mrs. Dryden was still in town, when everybody who belongs in this town knew that she had left. The reason you telephoned from the other room was to have Laymond and Andreth grab me at the hotel. But I got a message off before they nabbed me."

Fritz's smile was suddenly matched by a wizened grin from Tibbington. A gun muzzle poked Fritz's neck. He let his revolver fall; he heard Miriam gasp as he turned. The man with the gun was Laymond. He had come through the side door, bolting it behind him.

"Pack the jewels, Jim," Laymond told Tibbington. "We've both got to lam. But we'll leave them short two witnesses."

FRITZ and Miriam heard those dooming words. Both were tense, hoping that the minutes that Tibbington required would hold off the execution. The jeweler packed in a hurry. He was snatching up the bag when a rap sounded at the frosted door.

"It's Norgil," snapped Laymond. "He found the side door shut. He can take his dose first."

The swindler swung about. He never guessed that his figure was visible as a flattish shape against the bright light on Tibbington's desk. Norgil had been watching for that shape to move. The knock at the door was merely his first stroke.

The glass panel shattered as Laymond aimed. Through it came a metallic object, hurled with all the power that Norgil could give it. A big fire extinguisher from the arcade was hurtling straight for Laymond.

The big shot dodged, firing wide. Fritz hit him with a flying tackle. Tibbington clawed at Fritz, to haul him away; but all that was useless. As Laymond twisted on his elbow, to aim straight for the door, a revolver spat from the ruined panel. The swindler collapsed.

Norgil was standing over the wounded form of Laymond; and Fritz had Tibbington huddled in a corner when Trummel arrived with the detectives. The mainsprings of the jewel-snatching racket were dragged from their last lair. Laymond was taken to the hospital, where a dead body already lay as proof that he was a murderer. Tibbington went to join Andreth in the local jail.

When Trummel arrived at the hotel later, he found Norgil and Miriam at a table in the coffee shop.

"You spoke about a job," said Trummel. "We need another cashier at the theater. If Miss Laymond would—"

"Miss Laymond has already accepted an offer," interposed Norgil. "She will be a member of my company, beginning with next week."

"As the girl in the bullet-proof cabinet?" asked Trummel.

Norgil shook his head.

"Few tricks," he remarked, "have the distinction of never having failed. That cabinet, however, will be one with a perfect record. I have told Fritz to ship it home tomorrow."

Norgil smiled, as he added:

"No other audience could appreciate that trick like those six who witnessed it tonight."

Murderer's Throne

Chapter I
CROOKS HEAR NEWS

DEFT HANDS WERE moving smoothly in the spotlight, timed to the orchestra's soft waltz music. The hushed audience was like a huge, thousand-eyed creature, held spellbound. There was something almost hypnotic in the dexterity of those hands—the hands of Norgil, the magician.

Fingers plucked a cigarette from nowhere. Norgil placed that cigarette between his suavely smiling lips. He puffed it slowly; as the smoke curled lazily past his pointed mustache, he tossed the cigarette into the big ash bowl that Fritz held on a tray.

Smoothly, Norgil plucked another cigarette from the atmosphere.

To the audience, the cigarette act was a baffling performance; to Norgil, it was a matter of routine. Sometimes, he watched the faces of spectators near the side aisles, to observe their reactions to his sleight-of-hand, but tonight, his gaze had a different purpose.

67

Norgil's practiced hands were literally working on their own, while his eyes studied a group of five men seated in the lower box at the left of the stage.

The central person of that group was hard-eyed, heavy-jowled. Thick, brutish lips added to his poker-faced expression. With folded arms, shoulders shoved back square, he had the air of a king—that his thuggish companions tried to imitate.

Norgil had seen that ugly-faced fellow before; but for the first time, he understood why the man had been given his nickname: "King" Blauden.

A cigarette skimmed into the ash bowl; blandly, Norgil produced another. While he puffed it, he speculated upon the notorious reputation of King Blauden. The fellow was the local big shot; he controlled every racket in this town.

Actual crimes, however, had never been pinned on King Blauden. If Norgil's guess were right, King was responsible for the bank robbery of two nights ago, when ninety thousand dollars had been taken from the town's First National Bank.

All evidence pointed to an inside job. The crime had been pinned on Louis Lanning, a teller who had disappeared the same night. It was odd how Lanning, a drab, timid type of fellow, had managed to completely cover his tracks.

To Norgil, that smacked of King Blauden—though the law hadn't figured it that way.

THE music livened. Norgil's fingers were catching cigarettes in rapid progression; with both hands busy, he wasn't bothering to puff the cigarettes. Instead, he was talking to Fritz, in an undertone that only the assistant heard.

"We're closing with the Radio Vanish," spoke Norgil, "instead of the Protean Cabinet. Don't worry about music. I'll fake the tune-in on WKX. You can pull the news flash imitation."

Fritz looked worried. This was short notice; but Norgil's eyes reassured him. Fritz wouldn't have to ad lib his lines. Norgil would have them for him.

The final cigarette hit the bowl. The spotlight spread to a flood; Fritz was hurrying off stage. Norgil kept taking bows, following slowly toward the wing.

Fritz had already removed the Protean Cabinet from the full-stage set; and Irene, cute in her scanty costume, was stepping from it, wondering why the final illusion had been switched. Assistants wheeled a skeleton stand on stage; atop it was the radio cabinet that Norgil used for his new vanish act.

That radio cabinet was real enough; but it wasn't hooked up. Norgil had found it more satisfactory to pipe in his own imitations of current programs. Usually, Fritz made a fake station announcement and supplied music from a phonograph. Tonight, Fritz had a bigger job.

Norgil was still giving Fritz his lines when the curtains opened. He took a dozen seconds more, than strode on stage. He reached the cabinet, thumbed its dials. Suddenly, a voice broke from the loudspeaker.

"Express-Item News Flash service"—Fritz's brisk, nasal speech was a perfect imitation of the local commentator— *"giving you the late news early— Flash—"*

Norgil's right hand was reaching from the dial to take a cloth that Irene passed him. He was ready to cover the radio cabinet; but all the while, his eyes were keeping a side-long glance on the box where King Blauden sat.

"Police have a new lead in the First National robbery" —Fritz was snapping it, briskly—*"and if the tip is right, their theory exonerates Louis Lanning, the missing teller. Police see a link between the crime and local racketeering activities, which places suspicion directly upon one—"*

Fritz didn't add the name of King Blauden. Things were

happening with a speed that only Norgil could outmatch. The flimsy cloth was covering the radio cabinet; Norgil let it stay there, to make a grab for Irene.

He flung the girl ahead of him as he dived from beside the covered cabinet. Two of Blauden's trigger men were piling over the box rail, before the big shot could stop them. The radio vanish was cued to come with revolver shots that Norgil normally supplied. This time, others gave the cue—and their guns didn't carry blanks.

The driving thugs were shooting for the covered radio cabinet, hoping to cut off the news flash. They succeeded; but they didn't demolish the cabinet as they expected. Instead, they shot away an empty cloth, that Norgil should have whisked from the table.

The radio cabinet had vanished from the skeleton-built stand!

THE theater was in a turmoil. Amid that chaos, King Blauden made off through the curtains of the box, dragging along his other two henchmen. The big shot wasn't risking his own hide to help the two thugs who had gone berserk. Once they recovered from their stupefaction, they'd go after Norgil; and King knew it. He didn't want to be on the scene of murder, committed before sixteen hundred witnesses.

That murder didn't arrive. Norgil was on the move while the trigger men still gaped at the vacant table. Fritz and other assistants were springing in from the wing; they bowled the thugs to the floor. Orchestra members came over the footlights, to help suppress the struggling crooks.

Ushers were shouting in the aisles, to halt the panic. Spectators saw that the crooks were overpowered; they began to applaud that dramatic finish of the act.

There were calls of acclaim for Norgil; but the magician

didn't hear them. With the battle won, he had made a rapid
exit from the scene.

Out through the stage door, Norgil was on his way to
take up the trail of King Blauden.

Chapter II
UNDERGROUND EVIDENCE

KING BLAUDEN and his pals must have eased out easily
from a side exit of the theater, for they weren't worrying
about trailers. Norgil could tell that, as he followed them
in a taxi that he had boarded on the front street.

King's car was a big sedan, and it wasn't traveling in
a hurry. Every time it stopped at a traffic light, Norgil
saw the big shot lean out and give gruff but friendly
greeting to the cop on duty. Maybe King intended to alibi
himself later.

When the sedan swung from the main street, Norgil told
the cabby to make the same turn. Norgil noted that the
sedan was slowing near the entrance of an alley. He told
the cabby to keep going ahead. A block farther on, the
magician picked out a house address and had the cab stop
there. The driver pulled away.

Returning on foot, Norgil reached the alley and entered
it. He came to a small parking lot, spaced between two
darkened buildings. He made out the shape of the sedan,
hulked close to a building wall.

King and his pals were somewhere close, and it didn't
take Norgil long to guess their location. Near the inner
end of the blind alley, he picked out a house that was quite
as conspicuous as any sore thumb. That house had a doorway,

two steps down from the sidewalk, and the entrance was fronted by a rusted iron gate.

The gate groaned warningly as Norgil swung it. Unheeding that sound, the magician opened the door. His flashlight showed an entry, then a large room. After that, an inner room.

There was a door in the far corner; Norgil opened it. His flashlight was off, but he could sense the cramped space of a closet. He took a cautious inward step; then grabbed for the doorknob. Trained to quick strides and turnabouts that went with his stage act, Norgil was out of that snare before his leg had gone more than knee-deep.

THE closet was floorless!

Norgil saw why, when he used the flashlight. There *was* a floor, but it served as an elevator. King and his pals had used it to reach a subcellar.

It wasn't more than eight feet to the shaft bottom. Norgil made the drop, found a narrow passage below. Past a corner he came upon a lighted stretch. There was an open doorway at the left; the room was darkened. Ahead was a closed door, fitted for a padlock. King was probably beyond it, for the padlock was gone, and the hasp was swung clear of the staple.

It flashed to Norgil that here was a chance to turn a trap on King Blauden. Norgil didn't need a padlock; all he had to do was close the hasp and shove his fountain-pen flashlight into the staple. First, though, he wanted to see what King was about.

The door wasn't quite tight. Looking through, Norgil saw King and his two trigger men; another man, with wizened face and little, darty eyes. King was stooping above an open suitcase that teemed with bundles of currency, the swag from the First National.

Picking one bundle of bills, King pocketed it.

"I'll get rid of these," he said raspily, "before I forget it. You'll stay here, Bogo"—this was to the dart-eyed tough—"until midnight. That's when we lam."

"Ain't you gettin' rid of that?"

Bogo nudged toward a big box, in a corner, near the door. King stepped over, raised the lid. Norgil could see the light strike a dead, upturned face, that still bore resemblance to the photographs of Lanning, the missing bank's teller.

"We'll get rid of the stiff," promised King. "But not until after midnight."

Before Norgil could budge, King turned abruptly toward the door. His hand was almost on it, when Norgil whipped away. No time to press the door tight and jam the flashlight pen into place. Norgil's only bet was a quick slide along the passage, into the darkened side room.

NORGIL was in the room by the time King and his crew came through the passage. As luck had it, they stopped by the door. Norgil slid into a little alcove, just as Bogo entered. The fellow pressed a switch; lights came on from two battered floor lamps. One was near the door; but the other was in Norgil's alcove.

Flattened against the wall, Norgil could see a high-set window, covered by a drawn shade. He could hear King giving final instructions to Bogo.

"I'm leaving it to you, Bogo," informed the big shot. "If any boob shoves in here, give him the shiv. Croak any guy if you have to; if you don't have to, you've got plenty of rope here to tie him up. Then we can make him talk."

King and his cronies left. On lone duty, Bogo remembered King's admonition. He paced the center of the room, muttering to himself. His arm and hand came into view; Norgil could see the fellow fidget with a knife. Norgil tightened, expecting the shiv specialist to turn in his direction.

Bogo's attention was suddenly trapped by a chance flutter of the window shade.

It was just a passing breeze; but Bogo wasn't convinced. He shifted to the center of the room; Norgil could sense that he was still watching the window. The shade flapped again, lightly. Bogo grunted, resumed his pacing.

Norgil was already working with a prompt idea.

Unquestionably, Bogo was deadly when he had his knife. Without it, the fellow wouldn't be tough to handle. What Bogo needed was preliminary treatment to despoil him of his fang. His suspicion of the window shade provided that method.

REACHING to a pocket, Norgil drew out a lighted cigarette; a reminder of his recent sleight-of-hand performance. He tucked the cigarette between two fingers of his left hand, then cupped his right fingers above. The cigarette projected, as Norgil extended both hands to block the light from the alcove lamp.

Those hands cast a grotesque silhouette against the window shade. Deftly, Norgil found the range, to turn the shape into a life-size profile. Big forehead; flattish nose; pudgy, oversize lips—between the latter, the projecting cigarette.

Norgil squidged his hands. The cigarette puffed. Shadowy smoke flickered on the window shade. Another puff—a third; with it came the hoped-for flutter of the shade. Norgil could hear Bogo swing about. The magician's hands went downward.

Bogo didn't stop to reason that an outsider's profile would not show against darkness. The shape on the shade looked like a ducking head beyond the open window. It came up again, cautiously, shoulders below it.

Those shoulders were cast by Norgil's forearms, stretched to horizontal position. They were enough for Bogo. He had his target, there at the window. The tricked killer took one quick step, whipped his knife for the heart of an imaginary enemy.

The blade slashed through the window shade. The roller released; the shade lashed upward. There was Bogo, in Norgil's full view; the fellow's wizened face was as blank as the space beyond the window, where the knife had clattered.

Dropping the cigarette, Norgil made a long, hard dive. Bogo heard it, but was still too stupefied to even guess the direction from which the dive came. Norgil bowled the scrawny crook clear across the room; settled him with a hard thump against the wall.

Twenty seconds later, Norgil had reclaimed his cigarette and was puffing it complacently while he eyed the limp form of Bogo, senseless on the floor of the hideaway.

Chapter III
THE WRONG FINALE

IT WASN'T long before Norgil was on his way back to the theater. He had left Bogo, bound and gagged, in the room that held the swag and Lanning's corpse.

Norgil was due back at the theater to do his ten-forty show. The act would be off at half-past eleven; and that time, as Norgil reasoned it, was when the police should be informed of what lay in King Blauden's underground lair.

At present, King was probably probing the local grapevine, to learn if the police were actually after him. Premature moves by the law would merely be a tipoff to the big shot. The right idea was to lull King into thinking that all was well, then have a surprise for him, when he came back to his hidden headquarters at midnight.

Things were as Norgil wanted them when he reached the theater. The management had called in the police, to make sure that no new riot occurred. There were cops at the entrance; another officer at the stage door. When Norgil peered from the wing, he could see more bluecoats in the box where King had originally been.

The feature picture had twenty more minutes to run. Picking his way by the flickery backstage glow, Norgil reached his dressing room. A burly, long-faced man was awaiting him. Norgil recognized Detective Caston, of the local force.

Though Norgil had met Caston a few times before, the detective didn't appear very friendly. He put the reason bluntly. He had been here, asking questions about the battle on the stage; and nobody had the answers.

Norgil shrugged when Caston had finished.

"What about the chaps that started it?" asked Norgil. "Haven't you quizzed them?"

"They won't talk," admitted Caston. "It's clear enough, though, that you baited them with a fake radio announcement."

Norgil was seated in front of his mirror, restoring his makeup for the coming show. He watched Caston in the glass; their eyes met. Caston demanded:

"What about it?"

"The radio announcement?" Norgil's question was a purred one. "Just a bit of showmanship. Perhaps we overdid it. But on the contrary—"

Norgil interrupted himself to call to Fritz, who was passing the dressing room door.

"Leave the radio trick out, this show," ordered the magician. "Tell Irene we'll work the Protean Cabinet, as usual."

Rising, Norgil thwacked Caston on the shoulder.

"You see?" Norgil put it smoothly. "That settles matters;

there won't be any trouble this show. But stay around"
—his tone was confidential—"and I may have a surprise
for you."

THERE was a long-drawn call: "F-i-i-ive minutes!"
Hearing it, Norgil gave an apologetic smile. It was almost
time for the act to begin: Caston would have to wait and
resume the talk afterward. The detective accepted that
situation, but it didn't satisfy him.

Standing by the wing, arranging the fish bowls for the
opening, Norgil watched Caston snoop about. Caston
was looking at the electric chair, an item that didn't even
belong in the act. It was a piece of old sideshow equipment
that Norgil had bought from a retired carnival man. Norgil
had an idea that it could be rigged into a stage illusion,
and had assigned Fritz to make some mechanical changes
in the device. The job was finished; but it wasn't all that
Norgil wanted. The electric chair was to be shipped to
storage tomorrow.

The girls were hurrying down from the upstairs dressing
rooms that lined a metal balcony. There was the final call:
a blast of music from the orchestra. With impressive stride,
Norgil the magician went on stage, to face another audience.

All through the fifty minutes of that rapid show, Norgil
was thinking of the sequel that would follow it. He had
chosen the words that he intended to speak to Caston;
in fact, Norgil was repeating them to himself, while he
performed the cigarette act.

He could tell Caston that a hunch had inspired the
hoax with the radio trick; that he had seen King Blauden
leave the theater, and had followed to see where the big
shot went. That, and a little more, would be sufficient.
Caston wasn't a difficult fellow to persuade, if given
proper encouragement.

Norgil was right in that surmise. He was to learn how quickly Detective Caston could analyze a situation, when he had a chance to visualize it. Only the situation wasn't the one that Norgil planned.

Within the next five minutes, the suave magician was due for the biggest surprise of his stage career.

"IS Irene ready?"

Norgil asked the question when he had bowed himself off stage. Fritz nodded; the assistant pointed to the corner near the stage door, where two stagehands were wheeling the big Protean Cabinet from its place. Norgil beckoned for them to hurry. The cabinet reached stage center.

Norgil was out from the wing, as the curtains slid apart. He reached the tall six-foot cabinet, opened the door to show its empty interior. While Norgil stood aside, Fritz and another neatly uniformed attendant wheeled the opened cabinet in a circle, to show all sides.

Caston was gawking from the wing. Norgil twitched his mustache, to hide a momentary smile. It was Caston's job to solve riddles; but even from his vantage point backstage, the smart dick wouldn't guess the secret of the Protean Cabinet.

Too bad, Norgil thought, that he wouldn't be able to watch Caston's expression, when the dick saw Irene appear from the cabinet. But that moment called for Norgil to be facing directly toward the audience.

Norgil closed the cabinet door. He drew his revolver, fired two quick blanks. With a sweep of his arm, he grasped the door handle, whipped open the front of the cabinet as he turned toward the audience. He reached for the girl's hand.

A huge, indefinable gasp came from the audience. It carried horror, mingled from many throats. Above that strange choke, Norgil heard a clatter beside him, a thud as something struck the stage.

He turned. Irene wasn't there. Instead, a figure had rolled headlong from the cabinet, to stretch at the magician's feet.

It was the figure of a man, stiffened and grotesque, in his bloodstained clothes. That form from the cabinet finished its inert roll, with a sideways tilt that brought it face upward. A white, contorted face was staring with the sightless eyes of death.

Norgil's eyes were as fixed as those of the corpse. He was rooted motionless; he didn't even hear Fritz's frantic shout to "Close in!" that brought the curtains sweeping together, cutting off the audience's view.

For Norgil had recognized that death-stilled countenance. The thing from the cabinet was the body of the murdered bank teller, Louis Lanning!

Chapter IV
NORGIL'S VANISH

BIG HANDS were on Norgil's shoulders. Detective Caston was shaking the magician from his stupor. Slowly, the dick's growled comments were drilling through Norgil's brain.

Caston wanted explanations, and he wanted them fast. It was plain enough that he regarded Norgil as responsible for Lanning's death; but to Caston, the ways of a magician were beyond normal understanding.

There was just a chance, as Caston saw it, that Norgil could furnish facts to clear himself of murder. That dawned on Norgil, as he listened; but with it, he saw the hopelessness of the situation.

The taxi driver must have met up with King Blauden, and blabbed things to the big shot. King had returned to the hideout, to hear Bogo's story. The rest had been nervy work, putting Lanning's body where Irene should have been; but it hadn't been overdifficult.

With Norgil occupied on the stage, Caston and the cops watching the show, the crooks had found a chance to prepare their own climax. They had switched the burden of crime to Norgil, through planted evidence.

As for that other evidence—the swag from the robbery— it would be gone, by this time, from King's headquarters. There wasn't a doubt that King would do exactly what he had planned; clear town, taking his funds along. The big shot would be far away by the time Norgil could manage to clear himself from blame.

Norgil's wits were back. He saw one course: to locate King and have a showdown. There might still be time, for King certainly wouldn't have to hurry his getaway, under present cirumstances. There was a way open for Norgil, a risky one, for it meant that he would jeopardize what status he still held with the law.

Nevertheless, the risk was necessary; not only to go after King, but to aid a person whose plight was far worse than Norgil's own.

NORGIL was thinking of Irene.

What had become of her? Had she met harm from King's sluggers—or had the big shot carried her away? Whichever the case, Irene needed help.

"Come on, Norgil." Caston's growl was irritable. "What about Lanning's body? How did it come here?"

"You can solve that later," snapped Norgil. "What about Irene, the girl who should have come from the cabinet? She is the person who can probably tell us."

That struck Caston as logical. He didn't know how the cabinet trick worked; but since Lanning's body had appeared in Irene's place, the girl might furnish evidence. He asked Norgil where they ought to look. The magician suggested that they try Irene's dressing room.

Together, they ascended the metal stairs. Norgil stopped at the third door on the little balcony; he pounded there. No response came. Norgil gave Caston a worried look. The detective nodded to enter.

Norgil thrust the door inward; stopped short. Horror registered on the magician's face, as his eyes gazed toward the door. Evidently, the magician was shaken by some gruesome sight.

Viewing such scenes was part of Caston's business. The detective shoved the magician aside and shouldered into the room. He stared at the floor, puzzled. The place was vacant.

"Say!" rapped Caston. "There's nobody in here—"

The slam of the door interrupted. A key clicked from the outside. Caston was wrong about the room being empty. He was in it, to stay a while.

Norgil was hurrying down the steps. Cops heard his clatter; started to intercept him. Norgil pointed to a screen that stood near a wing.

"Detective Caston wants it," he explained. "It's the screen the girls use when they change their costumes. It's evidence."

That sounded sensible. The officers volunteered to help Norgil carry the screen. By that time, Fritz had joined them. Norgil gave Fritz a nudge, that the assistant understood. Fritz slid away, past the stage wing.

Norgil was at the screen, folding it from the other side. The four big panels were loosely hinged; he was having trouble with the screen. The policemen heard his voice:

"Here, you fellows, help me with this—"

There was a smash of glass from the balcony. The cops turned, stared upward. Caston's face shoved through the transom of Irene's dressing room.

"Grab Norgil!" bawled the detective. "Hold him, until I bust out of here!"

Two officers leaped for the screen. Norgil had begun to manage it, handily. Flattened shut, the screen lifted from the floor; its bearer swung it to ward off the police. He was zigzagging across the stage, poking away each cop who tried to flank him.

The officer guarding the stage door dashed in to help the others. The three made a charge, flattened the screen, with the man beneath it. They flipped the screen aside, to haul Norgil to his feet. That was when they blinked.

The man beneath the screen was Fritz!

Detective Caston saw that climax from the balcony, where he had made short work of the dressing room door. His vantage point gave him a view of the stage door; he saw Norgil, heading through there toward the alley. Caston yelled for pursuit.

From the street, Norgil saw the stage door gush police, with Caston among them. Norgil darted for a corner; there was a cab just past it. Poking in beside the astonished driver, Norgil shoved the man a five-dollar bill with one hand, brandished his stage revolver with the other.

"Get going!" emphasized the magician. "Travel—and don't stop until you have to!"

The rear door slammed as the cabby stepped on the gas; but Norgil wasn't in the taxi. From the curb, the magician ducked for a parking lot, crouched behind a parked coupe.

He heard the surge of passing police cars. Coming from the corner, they had spotted the decoy cab and were after it. Norgil's vanish was complete; he had gained his chance to look for King Blauden.

That wasn't all. Whether by luck or clever calculation, Norgil already had the trail he needed. From this outside corner of the parking lot, he could spot the hulked outline of a big car against the whitewashed corner of a building wall.

Again, Norgil had come across the sedan that was used by King Blauden and his hoodlum crew!

Chapter V
THE DEATH CHAIR

SHIFTING FROM car to car, Norgil took chances on spaces that lay between, to reach an old truck that was near King's big sedan. Easing up to the back of the truck, he gained a look into the big shot's car. The sedan was empty.

From a flood of thoughts, Norgil untwisted an answer.

King and his followers had been ready for their getaway, probably with Irene as a prisoner; but they hadn't had time to start, before commotion broke loose from the theater. Things had happened very rapidly there, as Norgil could testify.

When the chase whirled by, it had been policy for King and his crew to stay in their car. They had left it; but they hadn't come out by the street. That meant they could have gone by one route only, through a passage, back to the stage alley!

Norgil took that route himself. As he neared the alley, he learned why King had again indulged in a bold course. Everyone had dashed out with the police; stagehands, as well as the members of Norgil's company. Foe and friend alike were hunting for the vanished magician.

A lookout must have spotted that and passed the news

to King. In fact, the lookout was still on hand; but he had ventured down the alley, to make sure that the rear street was clear. Norgil saw the fellow at the alley's mouth. The man's back was turned. Crossing the alley, Norgil slid in through the stage door.

The stage was dim; from its vaulted depths came hoarse but guarded whispers. Guided by the sounds, Norgil threaded his way among big cabinets and tables, to reach an observation spot. He saw King Blauden, two toughs with him. Between them, the hoodlums held the limp figure of Irene.

"Where'll we put her, boss?" came the query. "In that t'ing where we stuck the stiff?"

King shook his head. He didn't like the idea of using the Protean Cabinet again. He looked about, saw the electric chair resting on a square, carpeted platform. He noted a coiled wire, then looked toward a square box that was fitted to a wall socket.

"I heard about this chair," gruffed King, "from the same guy that wised me up to the cabinet. He saw them testing it, the other day, and it shoots plenty of juice. Plug in that wire, then put the girl in the chair."

WHILE the crooks obeyed, King added other comments for their benefit. He was pulling a small packet of bills from his pocket, the same bunch that Norgil had seen him appropriate at the underground lair.

"The doll gets the juice," announced King. "And this wad of mazuma goes into Norgil's dressing room. This is the dough Lanning squawked about, when we put the heat on him. The only bills they have the numbers for.

"Explaining Lanning's body won't be all Norgil will have to do. Caston will find the doll croaked, and he'll pick up this hot paper. We'll lam with the eighty grand that's out in the car."

From King's figures, Norgil assumed that there was ten thousand dollars in the packet of marked money, that King intended to plant. That, however, was a minor matter. Irene was still alive; but she wouldn't be long, unless Norgil intervened. King was right—that electric chair could take real juice.

King pulled a switch to test it. There was a crackle, as big sparks lashed across the chair. King turned off the current; the thugs carried Irene to the chair. She settled there, limp; she looked tiny and frail in her abbreviated ballet costume.

Norgil had to get to the wall-plug box, fifteen feet away. The first stretch was risky; it was too well lighted. Close by was an upright rack, draped with costumes, topped by a Chinese devil head used in a quick-change act. Lifting the rack, Norgil inched it ahead of him.

The thugs were placing arm clamps around Irene's wrists. They thrust her back in the chair, fastened another clamp about her slender neck. They stepped aside, and King shook his head. There were other clamps they had forgotten.

The big shot himself stepped to the platform, to apply a pair to the girl's ankles. Then, from the front of the chair, he lifted the last pair of fastenings, to thump them upon Irene's thighs.

As King turned to the switch, three feet from the platform, Norgil came from a huddle in back of the costume rack. He stretched full length along the last space of floor, gripped the side of the plug box. Quick pressure of the side, and the box slid open, revealing tiny, hidden switches. Norgil pressed one. His thumb had just finished its motion when King yanked the switch by the electric chair.

There was a crackle as Irene's body took the current. There was plenty of voltage in that juice, for sparks zipped from the girl's fingers. But Irene's body didn't flounder in the clamps, as King expected.

Instead, her eyes came open. The current was reviving her!

NORGIL had pressed a transformer switch that cut down the current's amperage. Alone, the voltage carried no destructive power; but it made a swell act. That was why Norgil had bought the electric chair.

King ripped out an oath as he yanked off the switch. Something was wrong; he couldn't guess what. But there was another way to settle it. At King's nod, one thug pulled a blackjack, stepped over to take a swing at the back of Irene's head.

That blackjack never snapped. Norgil pressed the second switch that lay within the plug box. He reached below, to thumb a little dial. There were wild yells from the platform beside the electric chair.

This time, real juice was going through a wire, but not to the chair. The platform had metal beneath its carpet. This was a comedy number that Norgil had planned, to make committees from the audience hop about in surprise.

The little dial increased the current, and Norgil turned it past the usual limit. The thugs were jouncing about like chunks of human popcorn; they couldn't break themselves loose. Only King Blauden remained ready for action.

Norgil was driving for the big shot. The magician was aiming his blank-loaded revolver. King dived away, yanking a gun of his own. Both revolvers barked; Norgil was keeping King on the duck, so he wouldn't get the aim he needed. Meanwhile, those shots, when heard, would bring back the missing police.

With a sudden dart, Norgil came in under King's aim. He wrestled with the big shot; they reeled toward the platform where howling crooks still jounced about. There, King's hard slug made Norgil duck. The magician tripped, sprawled, with his back against a metal cage that contained a quartet of craning geese.

King pounded forward, slashing his gun downward, to take aim. His drive was unwise. Norgil's feet came up like pistons, met the big shot's stomach. King went backward, floundering, his ankles hitting the platform edge. By the time Norgil was up, King was down. The big shot had become another member of the dancing group upon the wired platform.

The lookout was in from the alley. He didn't see Norgil beside the cage. He saw King, though; heard the big shot's shouts, and spied the excited waves of King's hands. Then Norgil had him covered, before the fellow could reach the plug box.

There were foot-beats from the stage door. Caston arrived, with Fritz, followed by a pair of policemen. While Caston and the cops covered the platform, Fritz turned off the juice. The big shot and his pals came shakily from the platform, while Norgil released Irene from the electric chair.

WHILE King Blauden, handcuffed, looked on with ugly glowers, Norgil told his detailed story to Detective Caston. The bills that King had hoped to plant were in Caston's possession; so was the swag that police brought from the big shot's car.

The Irene episode brought questions from Caston. A charge of attempted murder was valuable, while the law still had to piece the facts that would prove King responsible for Lanning's death. At Caston's request, Norgil cut off the transformer; then, he pressed the switch beside the platform.

The deluge of crackly sparks that issued from the chair was proof that the unrestrained current could kill. It showed King Blauden for the murderous person that he was, and that revelation drove the big shot desperate.

There was a shout, above the crackles. Norgil swung, to see King breaking from the control of officers who held him. Swinging his handcuffs, King came clear, as his captured pals provided a wild flank attack.

It was Caston who met King, at the platform. They stumbled, rolled in front of the electric chair, as Norgil came springing into aid. Thugs were subdued; the police who held them were witnesses to the struggle's finish.

King and Caston were on their feet again. The big shot's manacled wrists were over the detective's neck; in frenzy, King was hauling Caston backward, toward the spark-ripping chair. Norgil had no time to reach the switch; and Fritz wasn't there to pinch-hit, for he was helping Irene up the stairway to her dressing room.

All that Norgil could provide was a hard punch to King's jaw, that tilted his head back, lifted his wrists a half foot higher. With descending grab, Norgil clamped Caston's shoulders with both hands, to slick the detective downward, out from King's hooking hold.

With Caston, Norgil rolled to the stage, in front of the platform. As they landed they heard a bellow that sounded like the cry of a wounded jungle beast. Crackles were muffled, when Norgil reached the switch and yanked it—too late.

Relieved of Caston's weight, King Blauden had gone backward. The handcuffs had prevented him from flinging his arms to save himself. He had landed squarely in the electric chair, to take the final punishment that he deserved.

Flayed by the devastating juice, the big shot lay tilted, half from the chair, as dead as the corpse of Louis Lanning which rested in an obscure corner of the stage.

Norgil, the first to reach the body, was the man who gave the solemn nod that declared the big shot's well-deserved fate.

King Blauden had found a murderer's throne.

The Second Double

Chapter I
DEATH POSTPONED

WHEN THE LIMITED pulled into Hampton, that Friday afternoon, Norgil's mood was as drab as the dull dusk that overhung the prosperous town. Staring from a window of the smoking car, Norgil indulged in mutters that were coherent only to Fritz, his chief assistant.

"Why worry, boss?" queried Fritz. "They're kicking off the baggage car; and the trucks are at the station. We'll have plenty of time to set up for the evening show."

Norgil tapped the ashes from his pipe. Stepping into the aisle, he hoisted his heavy suitcase. A wry smile formed beneath the magician's pointed mustache.

"I'm not worried about the stage," he told Fritz. "I'm thinking of those empty seats, where an audience ought to be. Booking this town on a last-minute chance was bad business.

"Steve Cragey thinks he's the best press agent in the world. He'd have to be what I'm supposed to be—the world's greatest magician—to fill a house on six hours' notice. We'll be playing to the rafters tonight, Fritz."

When Norgil made a glum prediction, it generally came true. The town of Hampton was to produce the exception to that rule. The first man to meet Norgil when he stepped from the train was portly Steve Cragey. In his chubby fist, the publicity man was brandishing a newspaper like the flag of truce.

Steve couldn't talk. Neither could Norgil, when he saw the front page of the Hampton *Evening Clarion*. The headlines heralded Norgil; columns teemed with news of the magician's unexpected advent. Norgil saw himself in a three-column cut, pulling a rabbit from a governor's silk hat.

"What do you think of it?" bawled Steve. He had found his voice, to shout above the hiss of the locomotive. "That'll pack the old Lyric Theater, won't it?"

Norgil nodded. He looked toward the street; then turned to Steve with a genial grin.

"One thing you missed out on, Steve," he said. "There ought to be a brass band."

"And I could have had one," assured Steve. "Only I promoted a limousine, instead. When you get aboard it, you'll find out why the town belongs to us."

The limousine was there. In it, Norgil met a tall, gray-haired man, the owner of the car. Steve introduced him as Claude Richton; and therewith, Norgil saw the light. Everyone in these parts knew Claude Richton, Hampton's big mogul of business, and chief philanthropist.

Steve didn't have to explain how he had swung those scare-heads in the evening newspaper. Norgil knew that the press agent had met up with Richton and talked him into cooperation. Since Richton was the city's biggest advertiser, the *Evening Clarion* had turned over its columns without argument.

"We met a few years ago," reminded Richton, as the chauffeur nosed the limousine along the street behind the Lyric Theater. "I remembered you, Norgil, and was glad to help. Cragey says you will have dinner with me, at the hotel."

"Of course," accepted Norgil. "I'll only be a few minutes with the manager."

They passed the corner of the theater, turned into the rear alley. Norgil noted that the little restaurant was no longer across the alley; it had been replaced by a shooting gallery. At the stage door, he alighted; went through the theater to see the manager.

THOSE few minutes in the manager's office developed into half an hour. When Norgil came down the stairs beside the lobby, Fritz and another assistant had just set the big display frames outside. Norgil was about to follow them backstage, when he heard a crash from the lobby.

A brawl had started, between two drunks who had stopped to look at the pictures of the show. The crash was caused by one of them hurling a display frame at the other. When Norgil arrived, the two were gathering the remains of his broken property. More bystanders were watching one man stuff photographs in his pocket.

Norgil pounced on the offender. The other drunk—sobering amazingly—came in with flaying fists. Norgil dropped him with a single jab; made a grab to stop the first man's escape. Something must have produced antagonism, for two huskies piled forward from the watching crowd.

It was a real brawl, with Norgil in the middle; but the attackers were taking the worst of it when Fritz and the other assistant arrived. The local combatants—drunk or sober—took to flight. Norgil told Fritz to replace the smashed frame.

When he rejoined Richton, Norgil didn't bother to mention

the fisticuffs in the lobby. Such occurrences were unavoidable with a road show. Norgil regarded the episode as unimportant. He was to change that opinion later.

They rode five blocks to the hotel. Norgil registered; sent his big suitcase up to the room. Richton wasn't surprised at the small amount of baggage. Steve had previously mentioned that Norgil kept his trunks and filing cases in the theater dressing room.

Dinner brought a new surprise for Norgil. Prominent persons were present, including the mayor, the police chief, and a newspaper editor. All, he learned, were coming to the show, as Richton's guests.

Time went rapidly, for Norgil, although he drank sparingly of the champagne that Richton had provided. It was eight o'clock when he arose reluctantly, with the remark that there would be no show unless he started for the theater. Richton said that the limousine was at his service; then he added:

"There's a special party arranged tonight, in the ballroom here at the hotel. We expect some seventy guests. Perhaps, Norgil, you would be kind enough—"

Richton halted; his squarish face was almost apologetic.

"Kind enough to do an act?" inquired Norgil, with a smile.

Richton nodded. Norgil's smile broadened.

"Count on me," he told Richton. "I'll bring the props here, after the show. Tricks that you won't see in the regular performance."

NORGIL was still chuckling when the limousine dropped him at the stage door. He'd met chaps like Richton before— swell fellows, who did plenty for you, but hated to request a trivial favor in return. Inside the stage door, Norgil didn't bother to ask where his dressing room was. It wasn't necessary.

Plainly shown by a backstage light was a door that bore

a large star. It was on the side of the building toward the alleyway, and a stone sill beneath the door indicated that there were steps leading down.

Norgil opened the door; he saw a light switch just inside. Pressing the switch, Norgil was rewarded with a glow that showed everything in place, as Fritz always arranged it, as soon as the show unpacked. The stage in this theater was built high; therefore, the narrow dressing room happened to be low. There were six steps down into it.

As Norgil's foot took that first downward step, his eyes fixed upon a slatted box in a far corner of the dressing room. The magician stopped at sight of huddled whiteness in the box. He recoiled, as if the stone steps were a live electric wire.

Turning back toward the stage, Norgil took one long breath, the sort that he could hold for a good two minutes. He went down the steps quickly; clear across the dressing room to the narrow, frosted window set in the end wall.

That window stuck when Norgil tugged at it. He had expected that result. The remedy was handy, in the shape of a heavy sword that Norgil used in the basket trick. Grabbing the sword from the corner, Norgil drove the point beneath the window sash. Thus equipped with a long steel lever, he used the sill as fulcrum; gave a powerful jerk that sent the sash clattering upward.

The cool air from the alley wasn't lovely; but Norgil inhaled it gratefully, as he turned about for another look at the slatted box. From this close range, the huddly whiteness was more clearly defined.

There were two objects; not one. Both were ducks that Fritz always placed in Norgil's dressing room, so their quacks wouldn't be heard on stage. But those ducks were no longer in a quacking mood.

As Norgil had surmised at first sight, the ducks were dead.

By observing them Norgil had postponed his own doom. This dressing room, with its low, confining level, was filled with poison gas intended for Norgil himself!

Chapter II
NORGIL PLAYS SAGE

BACK TO the window, Norgil lighted a match, lowered it beneath the level of the sill. The result proved that the gas was present, even though he couldn't smell it. The flame sputtered, finally extinguished, one foot below window level.

A second test showed that the draft from the window was clearing the noxious vapor. The next match kept a steady flame, until Norgil had dipped it within two feet of the floor. Stepping across the room, Norgil opened a trunk drawer, to obtain a makeup towel.

It was safe, by this time, to sit at the long shelf that served as a dressing table, and make up for the show.

Safe, so far as gas was concerned; but there was another matter that suddenly caught Norgil's attention. Naturally enough, he chose the end of the table nearest to the open window—and it was from this direction that the warning came.

Blended with Norgil's impressions had been the crackles of rifles from the shooting gallery, punctuated with the clank of tin targets. That background of intermittent sound had been altered.

There was argument across the alley. Thick voices intermingled with thumps upon a wooden counter. Patrons of the shooting gallery were starting an altercation with the proprietor. The muffled hubbub gave Norgil a quick flashback to that earlier brawl in the theater lobby.

The big mirrors along the dressing table were fixed on swivel hinges. Norgil swung the nearest one at an angle toward the window, which was almost at his elbow. He stepped back to the corner of the opposite wall. Looking toward the mirror, the magician gained a reflected view through the window, in the direction of the shooting gallery.

That wasn't all. His maneuver made him visible in the mirror. From an outside view, the big glass wasn't noticeable. Apparently, Norgil had placed himself directly at the window, to look across the alley.

That was what the brawlers wanted. There were shouts, an increase of the scuffle. From this confusion came the sharp report of a .22 rifle. With it, a bullet pinged through the window; shattered the mirror in front of Norgil's eyes.

THE clatter of the glass brought Fritz and a pair of stagehands. They saw the shattered mirror; bawled an alarm. Men pounded out through the alley, to stop the chaos in the shooting gallery. But their help wasn't needed.

Norgil could hear the roar of a departing car, that was carrying away the brawlers. Again, pretended drunks had started a near-riot; then cleared themselves from the scene.

When Fritz came back, he found Norgil outside the dressing room. Arms loaded with clothes, the magician was choosing another place to dress. Fritz's eyes bulged when Norgil nudged an elbow toward the box that held the dead ducks.

"Get rid of them," undertoned Norgil. "We'll keep that evidence to ourselves. I was supposed to be found dead, through an accident—either a gas leak or a stray bullet. We'll make it seem an accident that I'm still alive."

In his new dressing room, Norgil received a visit from the stage manager, who was honestly apologetic. It was plain that he knew nothing about the gas, and regarded the shot from the shooting gallery as a pure coincidence.

It was something else that bothered the stage manager.

"I'd like to know who stuck the star on that bum dressing room," he told Norgil. "None of the regular stage crew would have been dumb enough to do it. One of those extra guys must have been to blame. I mean the helpers that showed up with the trucks."

Norgil inquired if such extra helpers were usual. The stage manager shook his head. Norgil's late arrival had been the reason for them; but who had hired them was a mystery.

"Why don't you find out where they came from?" suggested Norgil, blandly. He drew a twenty-dollar bill from his pocket, as he spoke. "Only do it nicely"—Norgil's tone was a smooth purr—"nicely enough to make them think you were pleased; that we'll want them again, when we pack up. You'll learn more that way."

The idea suited the stage manager. He was so intrigued by the twenty-dollar bill, that he didn't notice the grease paint that Norgil was using. In place of the usual flesh-tinted No. 3, Norgil was applying the extra-pale No. 1.

NOR did Fritz observe Norgil's makeup when the magician met his chief assistant in the darkness of the wings. It was almost time for the curtain call; and Fritz had something important to report.

"Somebody got into your files, boss," whispered Fritz. "It must have been early, before they planted that gas."

"What did they take?" queried Norgil. "Lobby photos, mostly?"

"Yeah!" exclaimed Fritz. "How did you know?"

Norgil laughed softly. It didn't curb Fritz's alarm. The assistant gripped the magician's arm.

"You oughtn't to go on tonight, boss—"

"Don't worry," assured Norgil. "There's too many important people out front for anybody to try rough stuff from the audience. Besides, I'm playing safe."

Those final words were proven when Norgil came on stage. His entrance was shaky; his usually impressive stride had the symptoms of a stagger. Fritz was as stunned as the other assistants when he saw the pallor of Norgil's face.

When Norgil produced a mammoth fish bowl beneath. the cover of a large silk foulard, he nearly slumped before he could get the burden to a waiting table. Water poured from beneath the cloth, splashing the stage, as evidence that Norgil had let the bowl tilt.

Later in the show, the magician rallied; but his improvement was spasmodic. He seemed to acquire his usual brisk style, only through strained effort. Each time, his relapse made him look more weary than before.

In the finale, when Norgil fired pistol shots to mark the vanishing of three girls from a cabinet, he was actually supported by the faithful Fritz. Norgil didn't show stamina enough to stand; he displayed barely enough strength to tug the gun trigger.

The curtain fell. Norgil heard Fritz gulp thanks that the show was over. The magician's lips tightened, to hold back a smile. The stage show was finished; but Norgil still was doing the act that he had put on for the benefit of a special spectator.

Steadying his hand on Fritz's shoulder, Norgil stiffened as the anxious members of the company gathered about him. He wobbled suddenly; before they could catch him, he collapsed to the stage.

Flattened there, Norgil lay silent, motionless, while Fritz and the others bent over his seemingly unconscious form.

Eyes shut, Norgil experienced a flood of triumphant thoughts. Good enough to deceive his own assistants, this ruse would score with the man for whom it was intended.

Chapter III
THE FACE FROM THE PAST

PROPPED ON the bed in his hotel room, Norgil smiled weakly at the persons present. He felt better, he said, particularly since the physician had ascribed his condition to overwork and eyestrain.

"I'd been on the go heavier than I thought," admitted Norgil, as he adjusted a pair of reading glasses. "And you know, Fritz, I should have used these cheaters more often. That specialist was right, when he said I needed specs for closeup work."

Claude Richton was present. Norgil turned to him.

"Sorry, Mr. Richton," said Norgil. "I won't be able to attend your midnight party. Too bad you set it for tonight."

"We could postpone it," volunteered Richton. "How about holding it tomorrow night, subject of course to how you feel then?"

"Fine," agreed Norgil. He removed the spectacles; closed his eyes wearily. "And thanks, Mr. Richton, for the champagne. I'll have some of it later. It's just what the doctor prescribed."

Claude Richton left, accompanied by Steve Cragey.

Fritz began to work on the cork of the champagne bottle. He stopped, at a whisper from Norgil. To Fritz's amazement, the magician was bolt upright; all signs of his weariness had gone.

"Pull down those window shades," whispered Norgil. "Turn out the lights and take a peek into the hall. Make sure there's no snoopers. We've got work to do."

Fritz followed instructions. All was well. Norgil turned on a floor lamp; picked up the champagne bottle. Wryly, he shoved it back into the ice bucket.

"Two attempts missed," reminded Norgil. "Why risk

a third, until I know how I stand? I don't think this champagne
is doped—but it might be."

Fritz stared, agape. Then:

"You mean"—Fritz stammered, unbelieving—"you mean
that Richton is in back of this?"

"Who else?" inquired Norgil, coolly. "He worked the glad-
hand stuff too strong, Fritz, even though I didn't get wise
to it right away. He's working for something bigger than
a free act in the hotel ballroom."

NORGIL was poking through the suitcase. He brought
out a small projector and a box of glass slides. While he
was connecting an extension wire to a floor-plug, he purred
the question:

"You don't remember what photos were swiped, do
you, Fritz?"

Fritz shook his head.

"They were mostly old ones, in that frame," he replied.
"The same with the ones that were gone from the files.
You know how it is with those old pictures, boss. When
we run out of them, we forget them."

Norgil finished hooking a pillow case on the wall. He
turned out the lights and focused the projector on the
improvised screen.

"We're going to find that missing picture," he said.
"Richton didn't hear about these slides, because Steve
doesn't know I have them. Keep your eye peeled, Fritz."

One by one, the color slides showed scenes from Norgil's
show. The eleventh picture portrayed the magician placing
an alarm clock on a tray, held by a dapper assistant in a
blue-and-gray uniform.

"That's the one!" exclaimed Fritz. "That picture was
in the busted frame. It's a couple of years old, boss. We
wore out those old uniforms, two seasons ago."

Norgil wasn't thinking of the uniform. He was studying the face of the assistant who wore it.

"Jim Jorry," recalled Norgil. "That wasn't his real name, Fritz. It's really James Jorian. Where did he come from?"

"He never said," replied Fritz. "He joined the show in Duluth; quit at the end of the season. He had a girl friend there—Maisie Traymer—who used to be with the show."

Norgil remembered Maisie. It was she who had brought Jim Jorry to the theater. Jim had been a likable chap, and a good worker. Not the sort who would have a crooked reason for hiding his actual identity.

"Go down to the lobby, Fritz," ordered Norgil. "Get an early edition of the *Evening Clarion*. I want to see what news was crowded out by all that front-page blah that Richton put across for Steve.

"And pick up all the airplane schedules you can find. You may have to take a trip to Duluth, or somewhere. I've got Maisie's address. Hurry back while I'm putting through a long-distance call."

FRITZ was back in ten minutes. He had no trouble getting the early edition. It was the only one that still remained beneath the newsstand counter, for Steve had bought up all the later issues, with their news of Norgil.

On the front page, Norgil found the all-important item; read snatches of it aloud.

"Saturday midnight," spoke Norgil, "marks the time limit for James Jorian to claim his grandfather's estate. If not claimed, the six hundred thousand dollars goes to charities, to be chosen and administered by Claude Richton."

Crumpling the newspaper, Norgil hurriedly spread the airplane schedules that Fritz had brought.

"I talked to Maisie," he told Fritz. "She gave me Jim's address, in San Diego. It's a cinch that Richton tried to put me out—temporarily or permanently—so I wouldn't get wind of this business. The newspaper says that a search was instituted for Jorian.

"Probably it was; but Richton kept the findings to himself. He learned that Jim was with us, once, and it's a bet he knows the kid is in San Diego. Maybe the deadline is already past— Nope!" Norgil's ejaculation was triumphant. "Jim still has an hour to catch a transcontinental plane that will connect him in here by eleven-thirty tomorrow night!"

Norgil pounced for the telephone; he started his long-distance call to San Diego. Fritz supplied a canny warning.

"Maybe Richton has planted some guys out there," inserted Fritz. "If they're watching Jorian, they may stop him from making the hop. If you ask the police to start him on his way, those fellows will still get wise, when the cops show up. All they've got to do is make Jim miss that plane. A private ship couldn't beat that schedule."

Norgil shifted a sharp glance that proved Fritz's comments were unneeded. The magician had taken the mentioned factors into consequence. He had San Diego on the wire; but he didn't ask for the number at Jorian's address, nor for police headquarters. Instead, he connected with the fire department.

"HELLO, Chief Gilday?" Norgil's tone was cheery. "You guessed it right. This is Norgil. . . . Remember the honorary badge you handed me and said I could use, if I needed it? . . . I'm using it, on your identification. . . ."

Norgil gave Jorian's address; then:

"Make a quick trip there, chief. . . . Jorian's got to catch the last plane East. . . . Tell him I said that his grandfather is dead; that there's six hundred thousand bucks coming to him if he gets here before tomorrow midnight. . . ."

Norgil paused, listening. Then he said:

"No. Don't call me back. . . . If Jorian makes that plane, buzz Gabriel Farrari, who has the International Orchestra at the Coronado Blue Room. . . . Ask Gabe to play the 'Zenda Waltz' just before his finale. Tell him I'll be listening for it."

One hour later, Fritz was in the lobby, assuring Richton and some other late callers that Norgil had gone to sleep. When he arrived up in the room, Fritz found Norgil in an easy chair, wearing his smoking jacket and puffing his pipe.

The radio was tuned to a station that carried Farrari's International Orchestra over a nationwide hookup. Norgil was patiently waiting for a number to conclude. He gazed thoughtfully at the champagne bucket.

"I think Richton fell for my story," remarked the magician. "That bunk that the dressing room was stuffy; that those clowns in the shooting gallery merely made me nervous. From the way I staged that flop, he figured his deal was cinched. With only an hour or so to go, he wouldn't chance any funny stuff that might be traced back to him. Open the bottle, Fritz."

The champagne cork popped. The golden liquid fizzed as it gushed into the glasses. Norgil and Fritz sat waiting, until the orchestral number ended. There was a pause; then, from the radio came the tune for which they hoped.

To the dreamy strains of the "Zenda Waltz" Norgil and Fritz drank Richton's champagne, in a toast to the health and wealth of James Jorian.

Chapter IV
SATURDAY MIDNIGHT

SATURDAY DAWNED, with Norgil totally unworried regarding his own status. As a crook, Claude Richton was a conniver, the sort who would use violence only when necessary. Richton's aim in life was cash—not vengeance.

That meant no more trouble for Norgil; but it didn't clear things for James Jorian. If Richton knew that the heir was coming into town, he would do his utmost to block the bright young chap who had once called himself Jim Jorry.

Had Jorian been watched in San Diego?

That was a question that Norgil couldn't answer. If strong-arm men had been on the ground, they hadn't suspected that a fire chief's car had come to snatch their quarry and whisk him to the San Diego airport. There was nothing, though, to have prevented such spies from wiring news to Richton.

Norgil had carefully studied Jorian's route. The plane jumps were too long for Richton to reach out and institute trouble along the way. Unquestionably, the conniver had never expected that Jorian would begin his last-minute journey.

Therefore, the rub would commence when Jorian landed at the Hampton airport, at half-past eleven tonight. Norgil planned that nothing could prevent Jorian's arrival at the hotel ballroom, where the magician—as a final stroke of showmanship—intended to introduce the missing heir to an astounded audience.

Norgil dined with Richton at half-past six. Ostensibly, they met to discuss the midnight show, which Norgil was well enough to give. Richton, though, was strained. The bit of yellow paper poking from his pocket was all that Norgil needed to know why.

He didn't have to see that telegram to recognize that it must have come from San Diego.

NORGIL reached the theater early. He called Fritz to the dressing room; gave his assistant specific instructions.

"I'll only need the girls for the show at the hotel," declared Norgil. "You and the other fellows can go out to the airport. I'll have Steve there, with an extra car. When Jim lands, Steve will bring him to the hotel. You fellows can be the trouble-shooters."

Ten minutes before curtain time, the stage manager stopped in at the dressing room. He'd traced those helpers from the night before. They were a bunch of local rowdies; the same bunch who had shown up at the shooting gallery later.

The stage manager expressed the hope that they would come around again. He and the stage crew were unanimously anxious to take a crack at them.

"We've got some new recruits," Norgil told Fritz, as they stood alone in the wing before the curtain rose. "Tell the stage manager that he and his crew can go with you to the airport. Richton won't be expecting us to have a strong-arm squad in reserve."

The show was over at a quarter of eleven. By quarter past, Norgil and the girls had brought the light equipment up to the hotel ballroom, by a service elevator. They were setting props behind the curtain of the ballroom stage when a telephone bell tinkled. Norgil answered. It was Fritz. His voice came chokily.

"What's the matter?" queried Norgil. "Has something delayed Jim's plane?"

"It's not that, boss." Despite the assurance, Fritz was frantic. "The trouble's here—at the airport. The power line has quit. The lights are blotto; and they can't find the trouble."

Richton's work! The thought pierced Norgil's mind, with the realization that Jorian's plane would have to land elsewhere. From a medley of impressions, Norgil gathered snatches of new plans. He was cool, when he purred the question:

"Where's the nearest emergency field, Fritz?"

"Twenty miles on the other side of town," informed Fritz, hopelessly. "We can make it in half an hour, boss; but we can't bring Jorian to the hotel by midnight."

Ten slow seconds ticked, while Norgil turned his mental tailspin into an emergency landing of his own. Those seconds must have seemed minutes to Fritz. He was spouting incoherently across the wire, when Norgil intervened.

"You drop off when you come through town," instructed Norgil. "Let Steve go out to the emergency field, with the others along to cover him. Have him bring Jim Jorian to the theater; and then——"

Two of the girls had approached. Norgil lowered his tone. The rest of his instructions were in a buzz that only Fritz could hear. At the finish, Norgil raised his voice in a louder query:

"You've got it all clear, Fritz?"

Fritz had it, to the final detail. The glee in his voice was as expressive as his words. Norgil smiled as he hung up the receiver and returned to the ballroom stage.

MIDNIGHT neared. The ballroom filled with the invited audience. Claude Richton arrived, with the mayor and the police chief. They stopped backstage to see Norgil. While he chatted, the magician heard the slight rumble of the service elevator, above the tuning of the orchestra.

"Sorry," he told his visitors. "You'll have to step out front. I'm going on in a few minutes."

Richton and his companions took the hint. But the glance that Richton gave toward his watch was definitely intended for

Norgil's benefit. Only seven minutes remained until midnight.

Five of those minutes were taken up by the orchestra's overture. Curtains slid back; Norgil bowed to the wave of applause that greeted his appearance on the stage. Two girls were standing there; one at each side of an extended threefold screen. At Norgil's gesture, they wheeled the screen completely around.

Norgil was watching his audience; two members of it, in particular. One was Claude Richton, serene and confident. The other was an elderly, dry-faced man who looked bored. He was Ira Landenseer, the old attorney who represented the Jorian estate.

Landenseer wasn't too friendly with Richton. Norgil had learned that today, and had seen to it that the lawyer was invited to the midnight show.

The girls had closed the screen. Norgil wheeled; he supplied a pistol shot. The audience expected another girl to step into sight, miraculously arrived from nowhere. They gasped when they saw the person who did appear. The screen opened to reveal a young man attired in gray hat and overcoat. With an embarrassed grin, he removed his hat, to disclose a shock of black hair. He looked at Norgil; then bowed awkwardly to the spectators.

Feature for feature, even to his crop of hair, the man from the screen was identical with the youthful assistant whose photograph appeared on Norgil's color slide. There were persons in that audience who gasped their recognition, even before Norgil spoke.

Then, with one hand raised for silence, the other holding a watch, Norgil announced:

"Allow me to introduce James Jorian. And the time, ladies and gentlemen"—other watches were out; from Richton's pocket, and from Landenseer's—"is just one minute before midnight!"

Chapter V
RICHTON LEARNS A TRICK

APPLAUSE SWEPT that ballroom audience, applause such as Norgil had never heard before. Handclaps turned to drowning cheers, as spectators sprang upon chairs to see the abashed young man who occupied the center of the stage.

To the girl who stood beside him, Norgil remarked: "Wouldn't I like to have this in the show! Listen to the way it wows them!"

Despite that side observation, Norgil was prepared for something to come. He was stalling off as long as possible; but he knew that a stampede was due. Those citizens of Hampton wouldn't be satisfied until they had James Jorian on their shoulders.

Norgil shot a glance for Richton; another for Landenseer. Both registered. Those two men broke loose from the enthusiastic throng. They were making for the stage—and Richton was beating the old lawyer in the race.

That suited Norgil. He stepped aside as Richton arrived. Pouncing for Jorian, Richton grabbed him with one hand, while he clenched his other fist and shook it at the audience.

Norgil thrust out a warding arm, to hold back old Landenseer. The lawyer was close enough, however, to catch the words that Richton tried to scream above the uproar.

"This isn't Jorian!" screeched Richton. "He can't be Jorian! He's an impostor!"

There was a quick nod from Norgil. Spectators didn't note it; but they saw Jorian wrench away from Richton. With both fists clenched, Richton followed. The next move lulled the cheering.

People saw Jorian turn, poke his fist hard and square for Richton's wide chin. Richton wasn't expecting that punch. It took full effect. The word "impostor" was again on Richton's lips—when the jab interrupted it.

Arms spread wide, Richton landed flat, while the man who had punched him came glowering in, as if to take new spite on his prostrate foe.

IT was the moment that Norgil wanted. His face turned away from the audience, he supplied a loud, long boo. It was the lone spark needed to set off a new explosion from the witnesses. Hoots drowned the applause; there were shouts of "Shame!" at Jorian's attack on so estimable a person as Richton.

The crowd saw Richton try to rise; they witnessed the hard shove that Jorian gave him. Writhing in anger, Richton looked pitiable. Men sprang for the stage, to intervene. As the rush came, Norgil suddenly changed tactics.

Shoving back the first arrivals on the steps, the magician dashed across the stage, grabbing Jorian in his rush. With a crowd at their heels, they reached the service elevator. Pursuers—the police chief among them—saw the faces of Norgil and Jorian, just as the door slammed shut.

The fleeing pair were the first to arrive on the street floor. Though they had a clear route, they paused long enough to stare at surging men who came from another elevator. Then they were away, through a side door to a waiting car. The pursuing pack piled into other automobiles and taxicabs, to continue the mad chase.

Norgil wheeled the coupe through the back streets of Hampton, while his companion kept close watch on the pursuers. The magician was as tricky in his handling of a car as he was on stage. At a grade crossing, he ducked his pursuers by turning along the railroad tracks. Then, baitingly, he waited for them to regain the trail.

The ballroom scene, with the escape by elevator, had taken up ten minutes. Norgil used fifteen more with his zigzag tactics through the city streets. The trail was getting close; pursuers had increased, when he figured it was safe to force the climax.

Keeping ahead of the chase, Norgil found the street that led behind the theater. The shooting gallery was closed for the night; but he recognized it. Jerking the wheel hard, he drove into the alleyway. Other cars rammed close behind him. There were shouts when pursuers saw Norgil and Jorian dive through the stage door entranceway.

THE stage was deserted, but lighted. Norgil wasn't quick enough in getting his hunted companion out of sight. The police chief, first among the throng, saw the magician push Jorian into a large square cabinet; then slam the door and turn around.

They were grabbing Norgil, when he halted them with upraised hand. He silenced their angry demands with a cool explanation.

"Jorian lost his head," admitted the magician. "But so did the rest of you. I was afraid he would be mobbed. I had to get him away. After all"—Norgil's reminder was a smooth one—"Jorian is guilty of nothing, unless Claude Richton brings charges."

"Which I shall!" It was Richton who strode in with the announcement, followed by Landenseer. "Bring out that impostor, who calls himself James Jorian!"

Obligingly, Norgil opened the cabinet. From it stepped James Jorian, his attitude wary, as if he were ready to make a return jump into the vacant interior of the cabinet.

Norgil turned to Richton.

"What was it you called Jorian?"

"An im—"

The word faded on Richton's lips, as his eyes went dazed. Squinting at close range, Richton saw the authenticity of a face that he had doubted. Amazed, he gulped: "It *is* Jorian!"

Jorian was receiving congratulations from Landenseer. The lawyer's welcome made others friendly. Reluctantly, the police chief clamped Jorian's shoulder; turned toward Richton with the question:

"Want me to arrest him, Mr. Richton?"

Norgil was close to the dazed philanthropist. Lips motionless, the magician purred words that only Richton heard.

"No charges, Richton," undertoned Norgil. "Unless you want the truth told, regarding last night. Those thugs you sent, talked tonight——"

Richton didn't recognize the bluff. It was too plausible, and it struck too closely to home. He was anxious that no one hear Norgil's side comments.

"No charges," repeated Richton, hastily. "I don't want Jorian arrested."

A TRIUMPHAL, noisy procession headed from the stage door, taking Jorian back to the hotel. Criticism had turned to acclaim. The only man who still held bitterness was Richton, who found it wise to hide it. Fumingly, he stood beside the open cabinet until the parade had gone.

Richton was about to follow, when a smooth tone halted him. The conniver swung about, to see Norgil, alone, beside him.

"You wanted me to do a special show, Richton," spoke Norgil, with a smile. "You can have one—all your own. You see this cabinet—empty?"

Richton saw the cabinet. He watched Norgil close the door. The magician snapped his fingers; the door swung open. From the cabinet stepped a figure that made Richton snarl; a man who resembled Jorian in features. At this close range, however, Richton saw the faked facial contours that he had previously suspected.

"All right, Fritz."

At Norgil's words, Fritz peeled off the shocky black wig. He blurred the grease paint on his face, tugged away the adhesive strips that had altered his lips and eyes. With a grin of his own, Fritz feinted a jab at Richton's chin. Richton winced at recollection of the actual jolt those same knuckles had given his jaw.

"You were right, Richton," declared Norgil. "Jorian couldn't have reached the hotel by midnight. But Fritz could—and did. Fritz is good at makeup, when he has a photo to work from; and we still had a picture of Jorian.

"But we had to stall, and give everyone the runaround, while Steve Cragey was bringing Jorian here. Jorian used to work with this show—as you found out some time ago—so we didn't have to rehearse him for the quick-change cabinet."

Richton started to bluster. He mouthed that he would expose the fraud; that Jorian would never collect the legacy. With Norgil mixed in it, last night's events would be discounted.

"Go ahead," laughed Norgil. "They can take this cabinet apart, Richton, without finding anything wrong with it. I use it as a committee cabinet, to be examined by the audience.

"But you can't tell what you know without revealing too much about yourself. Maybe you overlooked the fact— but that monkey-business with the airport lights comes under the head of a federal offense."

Richton cowed; then, with slinking, sidelong gait, he made for the stage exit. He paused there, cringing, as if to deliver a whiny plea. Then, realizing that Norgil also wanted facts forgotten, Richton gave a defeated snarl, and ducked into the darkness of the alley. .

"I owed Richton something," said Norgil, in a tone of mock solemnity. "After all, he helped Steve get the front-page stuff that told people I was in town.

"But, boy!"—he jarred Fritz's shoulders with a thwack that suited the ejaculation—"won't tomorrow's headlines pack them to the rafters!"

Drinks on the House

Chapter I
TROUBLE BRINGS TROUBLE

AT THE END of the third night, Norgil was sorry that he had come to Titusburg. He could foresee that this week's engagement would be the worst flop of the season. Odd, too, because the Isis Theater was a well-located playhouse, and the only one presenting stage shows.

Steve Cragey had booked it on percentage, figuring the date would bring real money; and Norgil's manager was usually smart with such hunches. But this time, Steve had picked a "bloomer," as he'd learn when Norgil arrived in the next town, where Steve had gone ahead to do publicity.

By this third night, however, Norgil had figured where the trouble lay.

It wasn't with the theater, or the town. Those two presented a combination that promised a real build of business during a week's stand. The sour note was Lloyd Telfrey, who owned the theater and managed it.

Telfrey was a crabby, argumentative person who seemed

113

to have a lot on his mind except show business. He had turned thumbs down on every publicity stunt that Steve had arranged.

No advertising tie-ups in the newspapers; no free shows in shopper-thronged department stores. No placards in shop windows; because Telfrey wouldn't give out passes to those who displayed window cards.

As for the theater's own advertisement in the local newspaper, Telfrey had stingily limited it to a two-inch display, instead of the quarter page that he had promised Steve. The result: Steve's press notices had reached the dramatic editor's wastebasket. Which meant that Norgil might have received better publicity had he been in Timbuktu, instead of Titusville.

His show finished, Norgil didn't go to his dressing room. Instead, he told Fritz, his chief assistant, to wait around.

"I'm going to the mat with Telfrey," informed Norgil. "After all, we've got a contract with the guy—the one that Steve signed. I'll find more holes in it than in a Sweitzer cheese."

BUT the theater owner wasn't in his office when the magician arrived there.

From the appearance of the place, Telfrey wasn't coming back. Desk drawers were ripped open; papers scattered everywhere. The safe yawned wide; its contents—no cash among them—were in confusion.

Strewn clothing showed that the theater owner had packed a suitcase in a hurry. On the desk was a long sheet of figures, compiled on an adding machine. They were all that remained of the box-office receipts.

Norgil added up everything he saw, and calculated the total as a big zero for himself. Picking up the telephone, he called the backstage number.

"Telfrey has lammed," Norgil told Fritz. "And the dough has gone with him. Better break the news to the troupe, before they hear it somewhere else."

Norgil planked the receiver on the hook, spun about to face a man who had just opened the office door.

It wasn't Telfrey. The theater owner was a scrawny, undersized man; whereas this arrival possessed both bulk and brawn. He was wearing an ill-fitted tuxedo, with a lopsided bow-tie beneath his wide-jawed chin.

His square face had a big nose poking from the middle of it, and the wrinkle of his bulgy forehead seemed necessary, to keep his heavy eyebrows raised. His eyes were gray, like the streaks of his grizzled hair, and they had a hard glint.

"What's this about Telfrey?" boomed the big man. Then, his tone raspy with suspicion: "Who were you talking to?"

Though Norgil, himself, was tall, he had to look upward to meet the challenger's gaze. The magician introduced a suave smile beneath his pointed mustache.

"My name is Norgil," he began. "I happen to be playing this theater and—"

"With a magic show," interrupted the big man. "I know all about you."

NORGIL bowed politely.

"An agreeable surprise," he purred, "to find someone who knows that I am in town. If you will make yourself comfortable here"—he motioned to a chair—"I shall see you later, after I have attended to some business of my own."

The big man clamped a hammy paw on Norgil's shoulder, before the magician could reach the door. He shoved Norgil toward the chair.

"You're staying here," he bassoed.

Norgil raised his left fist, clenched, feinted a hard jab for the man's nose. Alertly, the fellow parried it. But he wasn't watching Norgil's right fist. It came upward at an angle of forty-five degrees, hooking for the best of targets— the big man's wide chin.

It was the challenger who found the chair; but he didn't sit in it. He took it over backward, to thump the wall beyond. Norgil didn't wait to survey the big man's crash. He couldn't waste time in a brawl, while there was still a chance to trace Telfrey.

Norgil ran out through the office door, down the steps to the lobby; there, Norgil ran squarely into two policemen, who grabbed him to ask the meaning of his hurry.

Before Norgil could explain himself, the big man appeared at the top of the stairs. Hanging on to his jaw, he bellowed words that weren't intelligible to Norgil; but the cops seemed to understand them.

The upshot found the magician in a patrol wagon, riding to police headquarters.

There was a delay there, while a fat-faced sergeant talked with someone on the telephone. The sergeant gave a nod; the cops walked Norgil outside and around the corner, to an obscure entrance at the back of the Titusburg city hall. They reached an outer office; beyond it, Norgil saw a glass-paneled door that bore the legend:

JAMES DOBAN,
DISTRICT ATTORNEY.

One of the policemen rapped. A mouthy voice gave the word to enter. They did; and on the threshold, Norgil forgot his suavity, to gape. Behind the desk, nursing a swollen jaw, was the big man who had encountered the magician in Telfrey's office.

"Next time you hand out a haymaker," growled a cop, in Norgil's ear, "pick some other guy instead of the D.A.!"

Chapter II
NORGIL BOOKS A DATE

WHATEVER NORGIL'S status with the D.A., he wasn't without a friend. Seated beside Doban's desk was a man who gave the magician a reassuring smile. He was evidently someone important, for his oval face was keen and confident, like the flash of his dark eyes, that matched his black hair.

Furthermore, the smiling man wore evening clothes of the latest cut and fashion. His perfect attire showed its merit when compared with Doban's rumpled tuxedo. With that contrast in view, Norgil no longer wondered why he had mistaken the D.A. for a rowdy.

Gruffly, Doban introduced the well-clad visitor as George Traymond; that was all he had to specify. Traymond was well-known as the owner of the Coconut Club, the bright night spot of Titusburg. Judging from the ads that Norgil had seen, the Coconut Club was making money with its floor shows.

District Attorney Doban began to state facts.

"This town is racket-ridden," he told Norgil. "I'm out to end all that. I've enough evidence in my safe to convict the small-fry crooks; but I'm holding it, until I get a line on the big shot."

Norgil studied Doban's safe. Faded letters announced it as the product of the Puritan Safe Co. That was appropriate, because the safe looked old enough to have come over on the *Mayflower.*

Safes and vaults always interested Norgil. It wouldn't require much of a kit to crack Doban's antiquated strongbox.

The drone of Doban's big voice brought Norgil back to attention.

"I have linked Telfrey with the rackets," announced the D.A., "and tonight an unknown informant tipped me to some further facts regarding him, enough to make it worth my while to quiz Telfrey. That is why I visited his office.

"Unfortunately"—Doban shifted his swollen jaw—"Telfrey appears to have received a tip-off of his own. That is why—to use your own description, Norgil—Telfrey lammed for parts unknown."

Doban swung his swivel chair to face Traymond.

"Regarding Telfrey," remarked the D.A., "I wouldn't class him as the big shot. Would you, Traymond?"

The nightclub owner shook his head.

"Not Telfrey," he replied. "He was a sourpuss, unpopular with everybody. Unless——"

"Unless what?"

"Unless all that was a pose!" Traymond exclaimed.

THE idea impressed Doban; but finally his slow nod ended.

"It won't do for the present," he told Traymond. "If Telfrey is the big shot, he can't afford to clear out completely. He's in too deep. We'll wait, though, on the chance that he sneaks back into town."

Norgil arose from his chair.

"And while you wait," he remarked, "I'll move along to the next town with my show. It may help business there, getting into town early."

"No you don't!" roared Doban. "The show can go; but you stay. We may need you as a witness against Telfrey."

One officer had a grip on Norgil's arms; the other was producing a pair of handcuffs.

"And I've got the way to keep you here," reminded Doban. "Have him slated, boys"—this was to the cops—"and lock him up on an assault-and-battery charge."

Coolly, Norgil remarked that Doban had begun the rough stuff, without introducing himself. That didn't carry weight

with the D.A.; it was Traymond's intervention that saved
Norgil from the hoosegow.

"I'll go bond for Norgil," declared Traymond. "So you
can release him in my custody."

"You'll guarantee to keep him here?" demanded Doban.
"For the next three days, at least?"

"Easily," assured Traymond. He turned to Norgil. "How
about putting on a turn at the Coconut Club?"

The idea appealed to Norgil. He and Traymond began
to talk about the type of act that would suit a floor show.
Traymond was pleased to learn that the magician had the
very stunt required.

"It's the magic bar," explained Norgil. "Not suited for
the stage; but I carry the equipment, anyhow. I pour drinks
from a cocktail shaker, any drink that anyone calls for."

"All from the same shaker?"

"Absolutely," Norgil smiled. "At least, it looks that way
to the customers."

Traymond asked where Norgil had last performed the bar
act. Norgil named the Club Lakeview in Detroit. Traymond
hadn't heard of the place; but that didn't matter, as long
as he knew the act could be done in a night club. He asked
what price Norgil wanted.

The magician lighted a cigarette, to consider. Then:
"One thousand dollars a week."

The price didn't astound Traymond. Instead, it suited
him, with the proviso that Norgil prorate his salary to the
number of days that remained. Seven hundred and fifty
dollars was the amount agreed upon.

Free, Norgil returned to the theater. He told Fritz to
pack up everything except the magic bar, and a trunk of
smaller apparatus. Fritz was to guide the company to the
next town, where Steve Cragey could take charge until
Norgil arrived.

"Miriam stays, though," added Norgil. "I'll need her to help with the club act. We'll have to give them flash, Fritz. I'm getting seven fifty—for a four-day stand."

Fritz whistled.

Two hours later, Norgil and Miriam were watching a limited pull out of the Titusburg depot, with Fritz and the rest of the company aboard. It was then that Norgil remarked:

"Seven hundred and fifty dollars. It will be a better net, Miriam, than we'd have taken at the Isis Theater, if Telfrey had stayed in town. But it's small change, for the job I'll have to do."

By which statement Norgil implied that he would startle Titusburg with a much more sensational show than the magic bar act at the Coconut Club.

Chapter III
THE FIRST NIGHT

WHATEVER PUBLICITY Norgil had lacked during his half week at the Isis Theater, the next day produced enough to make up for it. Norgil's photo was on the front page of the local newspaper, with a picture of James Doban.

Some smart photographer had snapped the district attorney off guard, with the result that Doban's face lacked its usual symmetry, thanks to his enlarged jaw. That photo testified to the newspaper story of Doban's brawl with Norgil.

Best of all, the newspaper gave Norgil's version of the combat; a fact which George Traymond mentioned, when Norgil arrived at the Coconut Club for afternoon rehearsal.

"Harley put that across," explained Traymond. "He's

my publicity man; but he works on the local sheet, so he's standing for the story. Maybe Doban will be sore; but he'll take out his grudge some other way than by slapping that assault-and-battery charge on you."

Traymond liked the magic bar act. The bar was a portable contrivance, on rubber-tired wheels. Norgil pushed it around the floor of the Coconut Club, pouring different drinks from the same cocktail shaker. Miriam served the drinks to imaginary customers; and Traymond, eying the trim brunette, voiced approval at Norgil's choice of an assistant.

Traymond was quite amazed by the number of varied drinks that Norgil poured. He sampled a few of them; then remarked:

"They're not as good as the ones that Jerry mixes at the big bar. Maybe you'd better let him do the mixing for you."

Norgil laughed as he clapped Traymond on the back.

"There's a trick to the mixing part of it," he told the night club owner. "That's part of the secret—which I can't reveal."

"You mean these drinks aren't real?"

"Quite real. Of course there are some drinks that are very much alike. Sometimes, I serve the wrong one, without the person noticing it. But that's a mere detail. What about the act in general?"

Traymond said that he thought everything was all right.

AT the hotel, Norgil dressed early. He wanted to get to the night club well ahead of time. Traymond was with some friends in the hotel dining room, but Norgil didn't stop to talk to them. Reaching the street, the magician was promptly spotted by a cab driver. He stepped aboard the fellow's taxi.

Three seconds later, Norgil was riding with the open end of a revolver close against his ribs. The trigger was controlled by a crouched passenger, who had been lurking in a rear seat. The cab stopped in a forgotten alleyway. There, the driver alighted with a revolver of his own.

Hoarse whispers informed Norgil that no fuss would bring no trouble. They wanted to talk to him; and the spot they chose was a little basement room, with photographs of prize fighters hanging on the wall. They seated Norgil close to the locked door.

"Heard anything from Telfrey?"

The demand came from the cabby.

Norgil shook his head. He figured that these two thought they could handle him because he had submitted to a pair of officers the night before.

"Whatever you do hear," spoke the rough-faced thug who had been Norgil's fellow passenger, "keep your trap shut. Get it?"

"Certainly," replied Norgil coolly. "I get it."

"And do what he tells you. Telfrey will make it right with you. That's all."

The crooks were ready to leave. Norgil knew it; but decided to make their departure one that would cause them to avoid him in the future. His left foot was close to the door. He snapped his big-toe joint out and in, three times in a row.

That was the way fake mediums brought raps from tables, thanks to the muffling effect of shoe leather. In this case, the thugs thought the knocks came from the door. The phony cabby yanked the door open, shoving his gun into the empty hall.

The other thug unwisely glanced in the same direction. He followed his own line of vision, bodily, when Norgil took him with a quick wrestling hold. The flung thug sprawled the cabby in the hall, where two guns bounced on the floor. The crooks scrambled for the outside door, when they saw Norgil snatch up a revolver.

Pocketing both guns, Norgil crossed the room to lift the tilted picture of a former heavyweight champ. He chuckled into the microphone that he found there. Norgil could guess who was on the other end of that hookup. He wanted the listener to know how he had fared.

THERE were two shows nightly, at the Coconut Club. The magic bar went over with such a wow on its first performance that the place was packed when the act came on again at midnight. The best patrons weren't at all reticent about calling for their drinks; and Norgil supplied them all from his amazing cocktail shaker.

He openly admitted that the contents of the shaker were limited; but when it was empty, he ducked behind the portable bar and brought out another container. Again, the magic drinks were pouring freely. Besides furnishing liquors, Norgil supplied teetotalers with such drinks as milk and sarsaparilla.

The show reached the point where there were lulls, while brilliant brains among the audience tried to think of concoctions that had not been poured. It was during such a moment that a loud-voiced waiter called:

"One Diavolo Fizz!"

For the first time, Norgil hesitated. The drink was one that he had never heard of. Then, looking past the waiter, Norgil saw James Doban at the nearest table. The district attorney was about to hush the waiter, when he met Norgil's gaze.

Clicking his jaws shut, Doban sat back and waited. Norgil approached; quiet persisted, while the magician poured a whitish drink from the cocktail shaker.

"For you, Mr. District Attorney," he told Doban. "Coming up—one Diavolo Fizz."

Doban took the glass and swallowed part of the drink.

He took another sip; this time, he practically gargled it. He shook his head.

"Wrong," announced the D.A. "This is not a Diavolo. It tastes like an ordinary Silver Fizz."

"Which proves," purred Norgil, his carrying tone heard by all, "that you are a hard man to convince—on anything."

The jest turned things to Norgil's favor. A few minutes later, the magician's act had ended.

"You covered it swell," said Miriam, when she and Norgil had wheeled the bar behind a screen. "Everybody thought so, except Doban, and he doesn't count."

Norgil looked past the screen to the table where Doban maintained a dignified silence amid the applause from everywhere. The D.A. looked quite satisfied with himself; confident that he had scored some sort of triumph.

"Doban does count," said Norgil. "A lot more than you suppose, Miriam."

But despite that statement, the magician gave a chuckle like the one he had voiced into the microphone. He had finished with the game of blind-man's buff.

Chapter IV
THE DEVIL'S BREW

EARLY THE next evening, George Traymond arrived at the Coconut Club to find Norgil standing at the big bar. The magician was watching Jerry, the barkeeper, while the latter mixed an odd concoction.

To certain liquors, Jerry added the white of an egg and a plentiful shake of nutmeg. He shook the mixture in a shaker, poured out a glassful for Norgil to sample.

The magician took one sip, then grimaced:

"It tastes like the devil!"

"Of course it does," laughed Traymond. "That's why they named it the Diavolo Fizz."

"And only a mug like Doban would drink it!"

Traymond laughed, then asked:

"You saw Doban this afternoon?"

"Yes," returned Norgil. "And he asked me a lot of fool questions, like where I was last night—as if he hadn't seen me here, himself."

Norgil paused to write the recipe for the Diavolo Fizz. Jerry read it over; nodded that it was correct. Norgil pocketed the paper. He turned to Traymond.

"I told Doban that he'd seen me," declared Norgil, "and that shut him up. So much so, that when I asked him if he was coming here tonight, he wouldn't say."

"He'll be here," promised Traymond. "He always comes for the second show. That's why I'm glad you're looking into the subject of the Diavolo Fizz. I was going to mention it, anyway."

He drew Norgil aside, where Jerry couldn't hear, to question:

"You're sure you'll be able to give Doban the real drink he wants? Out of the cocktail shaker?"

Norgil started a nod; then, he looked across the floor.

"Here comes Harley," he remarked. "I want to talk to him about some press stuff. Meanwhile, Traymond, take a close look at my little bar, behind the screen."

Meeting Harley near the door of Traymond's office, Norgil asked the press agent for recent clippings. Harley said there were some in the office; since Traymond had unlocked the door, they went inside. Proudly, Harley showed Norgil a whole scrapbook full of newspaper items, all pertaining to the Coconut Club.

There were other books that Norgil noticed; but Harley

didn't bother with them. They contained stuff that pertained to night clubs in other cities. Traymond filled those himself, to make sure that Harley produced his required quota. So far, boasted Harley, he had left all rivals well behind.

NORGIL found Traymond at the portable bar, examining an ordinary cocktail shaker, and still wondering how Norgil did such a slick act.

"I still don't want to be inquisitive," declared Traymond, "but I'd like to know one thing, Norgil. Last night, you gave Doban a Silver Fizz instead of a Diavolo—"

"That's right."

"But tonight, you'll hand him the drink he wants. Just how?"

Norgil pressed the end of the bar. A panel slid open, to show a row of empty glasses. With a wink at Traymond, he remarked:

"That's where the Diavolo Fizz will be. In one of those."

"But how—"

"How will I get the glass?" supplied Norgil. "I'll pour him a Silver Fizz; but I won't serve it. I'll pretend the shaker has gone empty. When I go behind the bar to get another shaker, I'll bring him the Diavolo Fizz."

When they walked out from the screen, Traymond was chuckling to himself. A clever fellow, Norgil, to duck behind the bar with phony drinks, and bring out real ones. At last, Traymond was in the know.

"I'm mixing the Diavolo Fizz myself," asserted Norgil. "Just for the satisfaction of fooling Doban. And say"—he stopped by the office door—"what about seeing Doban yourself? I talked him into returning that bond money. All you have to do is pick it up."

The news pleased Traymond so much that he offered to pay Norgil's salary tonight, before the show—provided that Doban delivered, as Norgil said he would.

That evening, the first show went over to perfection. While Norgil was setting up for the last show, Traymond joined him behind the screen. The panel was open in the back of the portable bar; on a shelf inside, Traymond saw a row of glasses with various drinks. The Diavolo Fizz was among them, conspicuous because of the brownish hue that the nutmeg gave it.

"Slide into the office alone," suggested Traymond. "I'll join you later. I don't want the other acts to know that I'm paying you ahead of schedule."

"I infer," laughed Norgil, "that you collected the bond from Doban."

"I did," returned Traymond, "with some uncomplimentary remarks regarding you. Doban said you'd picked up such a swelled head in this town that you wouldn't want to leave."

Harley was in the office when Norgil arrived there. The press agent had news, also.

"This is candid-camera night," he told Norgil. "And I've tipped off the bugs to shoot the flash bulbs when you hand the D.A. his Diavolo Fizz. Boy! Won't that make a story."

When Traymond joined them, the laugh was threefold, particularly because Doban had just arrived. The district attorney apparently expected to turn the laugh on Norgil, for he had brought a party of friends.

PROMPTLY with the cue for the last act, Miriam pushed the portable bar out to the floor. Norgil stepped into view, to take his bow. He began to pour the drinks from the cocktail shaker. At times, he noticed Traymond; and he caught the club owner's smile.

For the first time, Traymond was observing that Norgil frequently stooped behind the bar before serving the drinks that he had poured.

Norgil approached Doban's table.

"And you, Mr. District Attorney," purred the magician, "will probably want your favorite drink——"

"A Diavolo Fizz," declared the D.A. "I'd like to see you pour one."

A trickle came from the cocktail shaker. The liquid looked silvery; there was scarcely enough to fill the glass. Norgil stepped to the bar; from behind it, he brought a fresh cocktail shaker. But, as he returned to Doban's table, Norgil decided that the glass he carried was full enough.

He handed the drink to Doban, with the comment:

"A Diavolo Fizz."

"It's silver," the D. A. objected. "It should be brown——"

Doban was looking closer at the glass. He could see that the Fizz had a brownish tinge.

"You named your poison," jested Norgil. "Drink it!"

James Doban took a single sip. His tongue went rigid, following that taste. For once, Doban's eyes opened wide, with a bulging, demoniac stare. His whole frame riveted. Like a chunk of marble, the D.A. toppled forward.

The smash of the fragile glass was drowned by shrieks of women at nearby tables. On the floor lay Doban's huge frame, his upturned face glare-eyed—a portrait of sudden death.

That stiffened, grimaced visage gave silent testimony that the Diavolo Fizz was indeed a devil's brew!

Chapter V
CRIME'S FINALE

"DEAD!"

George Traymond pronounced that word as he stooped beside the floored figure of James Doban. Then, rising, Traymond pointed an accusing finger at Norgil. Traymond's shout was hoarse:

"There's the man responsible! Hold him!"

A dozen hands clutched for Norgil; but the magician was already wheeling toward the outer door. Straight-arming the nearest blockers, Norgil yanked a revolver. With threatening gesture, he halted Traymond and the pursuing pack; then dived out to the street.

Norgil jumped aboard a passing car; told the driver where to take him, with the gun muzzle as an urge. The car was away when Traymond and the rest reached the sidewalk, where they piled into taxis and parked cars. They overtook their quarry within five blocks; but all they found was a scare-faced driver. Norgil had dropped off along the way.

Soon, motorcycles and police cars were joining the widespread hunt. Norgil himself saw the last of the official caravan, coming from the city hall. On foot, the magician had reached the one place where no one would think to look for him. He was in the obscure doorway, where stairs led up to Doban's own office!

Ascending, Norgil found the place unlocked. He chose a deep corner in Doban's private office, crouching there, in the darkness. Wailing sirens faded. In the quiet, Norgil heard a sound close by.

Someone was creeping in from the stairway. The intruder reached the inner office. He lowered the window shades. Creeping across the room, he turned the gleam of an electric lantern against the safe front. Norgil watched quick hands go to work, but he couldn't see the face above them.

Fingers found the combination; the safe swung open, its door away from Norgil. The hands were eager, when they pawed among Doban's papers, bringing them into the light. The man's breath was short-hissed as he found the documents he wanted. He didn't hear the sounds which came as the magician listened; new creeps from the outer office.

Norgil slithered his arm forward and poked a gun muzzle close to the face that he couldn't see. He ordered:

"Put them up."

Papers scattered as the safe-cracker's arms went high. With a startled snarl, the crook backed away. His quick kick was a lucky one. It sent the electric lantern smashing against the wall.

In that instant darkness, Norgil dived, tackling the crook before he could spring away. He locked with a maddened fighter, who had desperately managed to pull a gun during that brief interim. Norgil felt the cold metal of the weapon, and shoved his opponent's fist straight upward.

The door of the private office whacked inward. Someone found the light switch. The glare showed Norgil at grips with a foe, who was wresting loose, hoping to cudgel his revolver against the magician's skull.

Across Norgil's shoulder, the crook saw the man who leveled a gun from the doorway. It was sight of the arrival—not the weapon—that made Norgil's adversary settle limply to the floor. Yanking the revolver from the crook's fist, Norgil hauled his paralyzed foeman into the light.

The captured big shot was George Traymond, owner of the Coconut Club! All fight gone, he was staring toward the doorway, as if Norgil had materialized a ghost.

There, waiting with leveled gun, stood James Doban, the supposedly dead district attorney!

The hunt for Norgil had ended when they reached the Coconut Club, with Traymond a dejected, hand-cuffed prisoner. Miriam wheeled the magic bar into the office. On the flat mahogany top, Norgil placed scrapbooks and letters brought from Traymond's desk.

"You had to get rid of Doban," Norgil told Traymond, "and you figured that his sudden death would give you a chance to raid his office and get the evidence that he held there.

"You saw a way to murder. Poison, with an almond taste, wouldn't be noticed in the drink that Doban ordered whenever he came here. But you needed someone else— an innocent person—to serve him a poisoned Diavolo Fizz."

Norgil opened the scrapbook that contained out-of-town clippings. Traymond had been forced to keep it, rather than have his publicity man wonder what had become of it. Norgil pointed to clippings from a Detroit newspaper.

"You knew about my bar act," said the magician. "You saw your opportunity, Traymond, when I arrived in town. Whether Telfrey was in the racket, or whether you intimidated him, is something we'll find out later. Anyway, you got him out of town, so I would take your offer to work here."

Norgil didn't mention how Traymond had framed him further, by ordering thugs to take him to an old meeting place that Doban had wired in order to listen in on small-fry members of the racket ring. The magician was coming to something more important.

"You knew the night club business, Traymond," continued Norgil. "But you were one man who had never heard of the Club Lakeview in Detroit. That made me wonder, until you met my price for an act you'd never seen.

"And seven hundred and fifty, Traymond, was away above the right price for only four nights, in a spot that's open seven days a week. You wanted me too much. This letter proves it—a report that you received from Detroit, regarding my act, with mention of the salary that I received there."

Scowling, Traymond lifted to his feet, gesturing with his manacled hands.

"What does this prove?" he demanded. "Where's any evidence that I tried to poison Doban?"

SMILINGLY, Norgil slid open the panel in the back of the magic bar. Traymond stared at the row of glasses that he saw there, all filled and untouched, with the Diavolo Fizz among them!

"That wasn't the way the trick was worked," informed Norgil. "You hired me to pour different drinks from a shaker; and that's exactly where they came from. I gave Doban the same old Silver Fizz, with a little nutmeg in it.

"You snooped around to learn my method, so I faked one for your benefit. The sort that would make you show your hand. The poison is still in that glass, Traymond. I had Miriam watching, to see you put it there, when you sent me to your office."

Traymond lunged toward the bar. He grabbed the incriminating cocktail glass, hoping to smash it. Norgil's hands clapped tight on Traymond's; the big shot couldn't break the grip, for his wrists were cuffed.

He managed, though, to thrust his lips toward the glass. As a last resort, he would gladly have quaffed the poison. Twisting sideways, Norgil gave an upward elbow jolt that caught Traymond's chin. When the crook's head went backward, his suicide attempt was ended.

Others had hold of him a few seconds later. Overpowered, Traymond lost the glass, its contents only partly spilled. Norgil had his last glimpse of the unmasked big shot when two detectives hauled Traymond from the office, to begin his trip to city hall.

Norgil was shaking hands with Doban, when Miriam began a question:

"But how——"

"How did Mr. Doban happen to collapse?" said Norgil. "He and I framed that little stunt this afternoon, when I stopped in his office. He liked my theory regarding Traymond. We agreed that a fake death would bring Traymond's final move."

"And you even showed me how to fall," boomed the D.A., clapping his big hand on Norgil's back, "along with the fake act I staged afterward."

"The old hokum," nodded Norgil, "that goes with phony hypnotism. You pulled it neatly, Doban."

"The credit is yours, Norgil. You thought of everything in advance of——"

The D.A. halted. He was watching the magician count a fat roll of bills that he had taken from his pocket. It totaled the exact sum of seven hundred and fifty dollars. The tally finished, Norgil completed Doban's interrupted sentence.

"Everything in advance," supplied Norgil. "Including my salary, when a chap like Traymond owes it."

Chinaman's Chance

THE BANNERS outside the Crescent Theater announced that the famous Chinese magician, Ling Ro, would head the bill for the last half of the week.

That news did not bother Norgil when he stopped to view the lobby display. He felt no professional jealousy whenever Ling Ro was concerned.

For Norgil, the suave, mustached American magician, and Ling Ro, the bland-faced Chinese wonder-worker, were one and the same person.

The Crescent Theater, the only vaudeville house in the city of Southport, was operating on a "split-week" policy. Business had built so well during Norgil's three-day stand that he had been held over for the remainder of the week.

The management had promised the patrons a completely new act; and to drive that point home, Norgil was switching to the character of Ling Ro.

There was a newsboy gawking at the framed photographs

135

outside the lobby entrance. Norgil tapped the lad on the shoulder. The boy turned around and recognized the mustached magician. Drawing a copy of an evening newspaper from the boy's bundle, Norgil spun a nickel in the air.

"Heads or tails?" he asked.

The newsie didn't answer Norgil's query. He expected the coin to vanish, but it didn't. Instead, Norgil caught it deftly, planked it into the kid's hand. The magician was halfway through the door when he heard an astonished gulp behind him.

The newsboy had just discovered that the nickel had changed into a quarter-dollar.

Norgil was chuckling softly as he went through the theater, where a matinee audience was watching the feature picture. The house was well filled; Norgil gave it the once-over while he paused by the sliding door that led backstage.

The magician reached his dressing room. He found Fritz waiting there. Usually Fritz wore a natty red uniform with rows of brass buttons; but today he was attired in gaudy Chinese robes that suited the chief assistant of Ling Ro.

"Better hurry, boss," urged Fritz. "The picture is running ten minutes shorter than expected. That will put us on ahead of schedule."

Norgil changed into his Chinese costume, with Fritz aiding him. It was not a long process, for he needed very little time for facial makeup. He dabbed his chin and jaws with yellow flesh paint, covered his own mustache with a fiendish-looking Chinese mustachio. Then, over eyes and nose, he placed a half-mask that was topped by a baldish Chinese wig.

"A good crowd out front," Norgil told Fritz. "They'll be packing the aisles at the evening show. The newspapers must have given us a good sendoff. Let's see what this one says——"

Norgil was thumbing the newspaper that lay on the dressing table. He stopped abruptly, without turning a page. Then, tensely:

"Lock the door, Fritz!"

FRITZ obeyed. Turning, he saw the headline to which Norgil pointed. It announced the death of James Birdley, prominent Southport jeweler, in an automobile accident while on his way to the local airport.

The accident was stop-press news. It had occurred only a few hours before.

"You knew Birdley well!" exclaimed Fritz. "Why, you were talking to him last night, just after the show——"

The assistant stopped. He couldn't see the expression on Norgil's face, for the Chinese mask covered it. But he knew the magician well enough to sense something from the way that Norgil's yellow-dyed chin had buried in his long-fingered hand.

"Do you think"—Fritz spoke in a disjointed undertone— "that maybe—— Well, that it wasn't just an accident?"

"Watch the transom, Fritz."

The magician's voice was brisk and emphatic. Again Fritz obeyed. While the assistant watched, Norgil stepped to a large trunk in the corner of the room. He reached into a drawer and probed the inteior. There was a slight *click* that even Fritz did not hear.

Norgil returned to the dressing table, carrying a pouch strapped to a belt. He whispered to Fritz. The assistant watched a trickle of gems come from the bag, to form a sparkling mass that nearly overflowed from Norgil's long hand.

"Birdley gave me these," informed Norgil grimly, "to take to New York for him. They've been bought and paid for—a hundred thousand dollars—with delivery promised before next Wednesday. Birdley asked me to deliver them because he was suspicious of somebody."

"And whoever it was," put in Fritz, "framed that accident today, hoping to get the jewels—"

"We can't be sure of that," interposed Norgil. "Birdley feared theft, not murder. What we *do* know is that anyone seeking these gems has found out that Birdley didn't have them with him; and if such a person guesses that I have them, he will realize that my position might be hard to explain."

Norgil was pouring the gems back into the pouch. Fritz was too tense to remember his duty—that of watching the transom. A yellow face poked into sight; darting eyes saw the gleaming gems. The spy watched Norgil strap the belt beneath his Chinese robe.

"Birdley feared theft," purred Norgil coolly. "Under the circumstances, I should be prepared to prevent the same—perhaps more. Tell me, Fritz, what about those extra assistants you hired for the Chinese act? Any of them look phony?"

"There's one I don't like." replied Fritz. "That fellow Herkin. I'll keep an eye on him."

The mention of the name, plus Fritz's intention, produced an electrical effect upon the spy at the transom. His face, shiny with its yellow makeup, took a sudden bob from view. A moment later a call came from the stage:

"Fi-i-ive minutes—"

THERE was a stir inside the dressing room. Outside the door, Herkin hurriedly placed a chair aside. He squeezed past a row of cabinets and other props in order to be out of sight when Norgil and Fritz arrived.

Managing that successfully, Herkin saw a clear path to a little anteroom that marked the stage door leading to a back alley. His exotic costume gave him the appearance of a Chinese assassin as he performed a slinky trip in that direction.

There was no one on duty at the stage door. Closed in the little anteroom, Herkin plunked a nickel in the pay box of the backstage telephone. He dialed a number, recognized the voice that came promptly from the receiver.

"I spotted the sparklers," informed Herkin in a raspy whisper. "Norgil has got 'em on him. You'd better get down here while the show's on, chief. You'll have a chance to sound him out afterward."

That ended the conversation. With a wise smile on his made-up face, Herkin slid in from the anteroom and joined the troupe on stage.

While Norgil was busy with his final preparations, Fritz was posting the other assistants and had run into some slight complications. By the time Fritz had straightened matters out, Herkin was in his own place. The assistant noticed him there, and didn't guess that Herkin had been late in arriving on the stage.

The finish of the overture was followed by the curtain's rise. The orchestra provided a weird Chinese melody, while the audience gasped at the splendor of the stage setting. There, attired in the gorgeous robes of a mandarin, stood the Chinese wizard, Ling Ro.

On each side of him was an assistant, wearing a grotesque devil's head, while in the background were other members of the company, all in Chinese garb. Behind the masked face of Ling Ro were the features of Norgil, but that was something the audience did not see.

Nor did anyone in the audience observe the ugly smile that flickered on the lips of Herkin, the Chinese-garbed assistant, whose master was a secret foe plotting ill for Norgil the magician.

Chapter II
NORGIL MEETS VISITORS

THE CHINESE act was a vast contrast to Norgil's usual performances, though equally as good. As Ling Ro, the magician was bland instead of suave; moreover, the act was silent, pantomime serving in place of patter.

It was uncanny the way that Ling Ro produced huge bowls of goldfish from beneath a silken cloth, and caused quantities of rice to change into water.

The larger illusions also had a Chinese flavor. Assistants dressed as coolies carried in two square chests filled with tea. Scarcely had the covers closed, before Ling Ro's handclap brought two girls in Chinese costume popping from the chests.

Then, at a wave from the mandarin magician, the devil-garbed assistants inserted one chest within the other. Again a handclap; the covers lifted and a third girl made her mysterious appearance.

The finale was the most sensational of all.

Norgil had finished a paper-tearing routine in perfect Ling Ro style. He was working "in one"—in front of a curtain—which lifted to reveal a full-stage set. There stood Fritz and other male assistants, attired as a squad of Chinese solidiers.

The squad seized Ling Ro, stood him against the wall at one side of the stage. Gripped between his hands, the magician held a china plate as a target in front of his breast.

At the other side of the stage, near the rundown, the soldiers displayed cartridges, and loaded the rifles that they carried. They aimed for the fragile target that was Ling Ro's only shield. Fritz babbled a high-pitched command to fire. As he swung his sword downward, the rifles crackled.

The audience saw Ling Ro grimace as he staggered. Slowly

his bland smile returned. He extended the plate, unbroken, raising it on a level toward his lips. His mouth opened; a bullet appeared between his teeth, to drop with a convincing plunk upon the plate.

Another bullet followed; then a third and a fourth. All were accounted for when the fourth pellet clanked on the plate. The soldiers registered feigned amazement as the curtains closed, while Ling Ro stepped through to take his bow amid the billows of applause provided by the audience.

Reaching his dressing room, Norgil placed his hands upon the forehead of his half-mask, to sweep it back from his head, wig and all. Flinging the mask upon the dressing table, he began to smear cold cream over his lower features.

HE was thus engaged when someone knocked on the door. Norgil gave the word to enter; then he swung suddenly from the mirror.

The man who stepped into the room was bearded, which gave him a dignified appearance. That was probably why he wore the dark beard, for it offset the sly look in his slitted, heavy-lidded eyes.

Lips parted amid the beard to reveal gleaming teeth, displayed in a smile that their owner considered a disarming one. But Norgil wasn't fooled into thinking that his visitor was friendly.

"Remember me, Norgil?"

"Sure." Norgil accepted the bearded man's proffered hand. "Sit down, Bela Bey, and chin a while."

Bela Bey wasn't a Hindu; nor did he actually pretend to be one. His situation was something like Norgil's, when the latter appeared as the Chinaman, Ling Ro. But Bela Bey had been in show business so long that everyone called him by his stage name.

The biggest fake about Bela Bey was his voice. It was

raspy, although he tried to tone it into a mild purr. While
he talked, it became obvious that he wasn't interested in
what he said. Bela Bey was trying to learn about something
that he didn't mention; and from the way his sly eyes roved
the dressing room, Norgil figured that it might be the matter
of Birdley's jewels.

"So I chucked the crystal-gazing racket"—Bela Bey was
reviewing his career of the past few years—"and worked
a 'hyp' act for a while. Then I cleaned up on the radio,
giving advice to persons who wrote in at a dollar a throw.

"I was chased off the air, but that didn't matter. I'd
made my dough. And now, the way I figure it, things are
ripe for the crystal-gazing stunt all over again. I've been
sticking in this burg because I have friends here, but I'm
going South next week."

Fritz came into the dressing room, wearing overalls instead
of his Chinese costume.

"I called the hotel," he told Norgil. "Miriam is feeling
better; but I told her we wouldn't need her in the act tonight,
like you said."

Bela Bey left with Fritz. Seated alone in the dressing
room, Norgil mechanically undid the belt that girded his
waist, drawing the jewel pouch from beneath his Chinese
costume.

He was wondering just how much Bela Bey had guessed.

FIVE MINUTES later, another visitor arrived. He was a tall,
stoop-shouldered man with gray-streaked hair and a serious,
long-drawn face. He introduced himself as Claude Darriel; like
Bela Bey, he had seen Norgil's show and was enthusiastic over
the magician's impersonation of a Chinaman.

Then, abruptly, Darriel came down to business.

"It's about Birdley," he declared. "I was his silent partner;
but recently, he bought out most of my interest in his

jewelry business. There was something"—Darriel's tone
became cautious—"that Birdley confided to me a while ago.
A matter of jewels worth a hundred thousand dollars."

Norgil was changing into street clothes. He seemed in-
different to Dariel's statement.

"Tell me," persisted the stoop-shouldered man, "did
Birdley entrust those jewels to you?"

"He did," replied Norgil suddenly. "I am to deliver them
in New York."

Darriel looked relieved. Then:

"Are they safe?" he asked, his tone tinged with anxiety.
"Here—or wherever you have them?"

Norgil pondered. The question seemed to bother him.

"I have a safe in my office," suggested Darriel. "If they
were placed there, no one could guess. Later, when you
conclude your engagement here, I could return them."

The idea struck Norgil as a good one. From a trunk, he
brought an oblong metal box, placing it in Darriel's hands.
The stoop-shouldered man observed that the box had an
intricate lock.

"The jewels are in this box," confided Norgil. "Wait
until I see if the way is clear. Then slide over to your office.
I'll join you there. I'd like to see the safe."

Herkin wasn't around when Darriel and Norgil left sepa-
rately by the stage door. The alley was likewise deserted;
and gathering dusk rendered their departures inconspicuous.

At Darriel's office, Norgil saw the locked box go into
the safe. After that, the magician went to dinner. Finished
with his meal, he had nearly an hour to spare before the
next show. Norgil went to the hotel.

The hotel room was dark when Norgil entered it. He
was closing the door when he pressed the light switch.
Despite the slam of the door, Norgil heard a sound from
an inner corner. He spun about.

Pointed straight toward him was the glimmering muzzle of a revolver. The gun was gripped in a frail hand; but the face above it was determined. So was the woman's voice that Norgil recognized, although the words astounded him.

"Raise your hands, Norgil. Don't make a move or I'll fire. I mean it!"

Norgil's hands went upward, while through his brain flashed the thoughts of treachery that he had expected— but not from this source. Apparently Fritz had been wrong about Herkin, the newcomer. Fritz should have investigated persons who had been with Norgil's troupe a longer while.

The girl with the gun was Miriam Laymond, the last member of the company whose loyalty Norgil would have questioned!

Chapter III
THE GAME THAT FAILED

MIRIAM HADN'T been waiting alone for Norgil. Hardly had the magician raised his hands, before three men stepped into sight; one from a closet, two from the doorway of an inner room.

All had guns. They were wearing bandana masks; but from their growled tones, it was plain that they were thuggish gentry. How Miriam had happened to team up with this gang was a mystery to Norgil, but only for a few minutes.

The girl watched while they were binding the magician. There was anxiety on her face when they thrust a gag between the magician's jaws. Miriam drew closer, as if in timid protest. That was when Norgil gained a closer look at her gun.

There wasn't a cartridge in the revolver.

Plainly the thugs had trapped Miriam beforehand. They had threatened her with death, and the same to Norgil, if she did not play the part of stooge. The whole game was a hoax to make Norgil blame Miriam afterward.

Of the two evils, Miriam had accepted the one that she wisely considered to be lesser. She had hoped, perhaps, to give Norgil a warning when he entered the hotel room, but he had let the door close too soon.

Two guns had been covering him from doorways, and a third had been trained upon Miriam. So she had gamely gone ahead, to lull the crooks into thinking she wouldn't trick them. Her present hope was that of helping Norgil later.

Two thugs carried Norgil down a fire tower, while the third followed with Miriam. Ostensibly, the girl was still the leader, for Norgil heard her whisper orders; but he knew that those words were inspired by the hoodlum who was close at Miriam's side.

All the while Norgil was hoping for a quick break. When they reached the bottom of the fire tower, he saw his chance. As he was hauled toward a parking lot beside the hotel, he took a quick shoulder glance and saw Miriam stepping back into the fire tower.

The thug who accompanied the girl was looking elsewhere. He didn't notice that Miriam had eased away. This was one place where gunfire would be risky. Norgil acted on that hunch.

Twisting, he threw his weight against the man on his right. Heaving forward, he drove his head straight for the jaw of the fellow on the left. That jolt was as solid as a punch. The crook went flat, and Norgil, bound hand and foot, sprawled with him.

Rolling on his back, Norgil came up with his feet to meet the other man's lunge. The stroke was perfect; he catapulted the fellow half a dozen feet, knocking the wind out of him. But that success proved the finish of Norgil's efforts.

A man sprang from a parked car, sledged a gun for Norgil's head. The magician ducked, but couldn't ward off the blow. His head seemed to split with a blinding flash; and in that last instant, he saw Miriam smothered by the masked crook at the fire tower.

WHEN Norgil awoke, he was lying on a rough wooden floor in a dimly lighted, shuttered room. He was no longer gagged, and his bonds had been changed. He was spread-eagled, and ropes from his ankles and wrists led to two objects that looked like clothes-wringers: one at his feet, the other at his head.

Miriam was standing close by, holding the empty gun. One of the thugs nudged her. Miriam spoke.

"You're going to talk," she told Norgil, steadily. "You'll tell us all about Birdley's jewels, or we'll turn the wringers—in opposite directions."

"And you'll stretch," added a thug, thrusting his blocky jaw from beneath his bandana. "More than the ropes will."

Norgil began to talk. His words were a babble that seemed like a plea. The thugs listened carefully, but caught nothing. Miriam was the only one who did.

Among those words were cues that Norgil had taught her for a mind-reading act that he intended to work at club shows. Out of the jargon, Miriam was receiving coded statements that she understood.

"Get a gun—"

That was the first statement, and Miriam returned a slight nod. She had a gun already, but she knew that it wasn't loaded. Norgil hoped that she could find a way to switch guns with a thug.

"Leave me alone—"

Norgil's second message also promised results. Miriam knew how clever Norgil was at escapes. Though the thugs thought they had him in a hopeless predicament, the situation might prove otherwise.

Another nod from Miriam. Norgil's words ended; his eyes closed. The thugs drew into a huddle, taking Miriam with them. Norgil could overhear the conversation. Miriam was coolly promising to make Norgil talk if the thugs would cut her in on a share of the jewel money.

The girl's bluff worked. The thugs let her take charge. She pointed to the wringers with her gun. Two crooks took the handles, and one did exactly what Miriam hoped. He laid his revolver on a table in the corner.

The wringers were unclamped, the crooks waiting for Miriam's next order. Drawing close behind the thug at the lower wringer, Miriam slid her hand behind his back. When her hand came into view again, it still had a gun; but she had swapped her empty weapon for the loaded one.

"No use." Miriam shook her head as she eyed Norgil. "I saw him groggy once before. We'll have to give him a while to come around. After that, it will be easy."

The thugs tightened the clamps. Again they buzzed in conference. Miriam gesticulated toward Norgil, murmuring that she didn't want him to overhear. By mutual consent, the group went into another room, closing the door behind them.

It was then that Norgil went to work.

CROOKS had said that he would stretch, and he did. He clutched the ropes above his wrists, pulled himself in that direction. The lower ropes lengthened slightly, which was a help, but the greatest stretch was Norgil's own. His shoulders wrenched; his knees went almost from their joints. His ankles, too, took their share of self-inflicted torture of the sort that crooks intended to give him later.

Amid the grueling pain, Norgil's numbed fingers found the upper wringer and crawled for the clamp. The cold metal gave them action. His fingers pressed; the clamp released. Norgil let his body relax. A dozen seconds relieved the nausea that had gripped him.

Using his elbows as props, Norgil sat up. The loosened wringer unrolled, giving all the slack he needed. Bringing his hands together, he undid the knots. Reaching forward, he soon settled the ankle ropes.

Freed, Norgil stole to the door. It opened in the other direction. Norgil pressed it inward and peering, he saw Miriam talking with three of the hoodlums. The fourth was absent, a fact that inspired Norgil to immediate action, for he didn't know how soon the fellow might return.

Norgil shoved the door half open. The crooks heard the clatter and whipped about. The nearest man made a dive for the door, aiming his gun as Norgil whipped the barrier shut. That was a double ruse. Before the crook reached the door, it swung open again with all the force that Norgil could give it.

The door took the thug head-on; it felled him to the center of the outside room.

Miriam was covering the other pair, telling them her gun was loaded. They didn't believe her. One crook made a grab for her and the girl had to fire. The crook sagged; his revolver dropped, for the bullet had found the shoulder of his gun arm. But he still put up a struggle.

The last thug was driving for Norgil, aiming point-blank. He tugged the trigger as he came. But Norgil remained immune, as he had been in his bullet-catching act. He floored the attacker with a series of quick punches; then hauled away the wounded thug who battled Miriam.

The girl gasped, wondering at her rescue. She had caught

a glimpse of a gun aiming straight for Norgil, and had considered the magician doomed. Norgil saw her bewilderment. Chuckling, he picked up the gun that the aiming crook had dropped.

Luck had played its part in victory. The only thug who had gained an opportunity to riddle Norgil was the one whose gun had been exchanged for Miriam's when the girl made the secret swap!

Chapter IV
THE SHOW GOES ON

WHILE THEY bound and gagged the three prisoners, Miriam told Norgil where the fourth thug had gone.

"They're working for somebody here in town," she explained. "They let that out when they thought I was on their side. They finally decided to postpone your torture until one man contacted the chief, whoever he is."

"How soon does he intend to meet him?" inquired Norgil. "Did you get a line on that?"

"He said he would see him after the show," replied Miriam. "But the man who left was the only one of us who had a watch. I didn't see the time when he looked at it."

Norgil's own watch was stopped. It had been broken in the scuffle outside the hotel. Miriam admitted that she couldn't calculate how late it was; and Norgil's own estimate was hazy, for he had been unconscious during the trip to this headquarters.

Moreover, Miriam couldn't figure how far they had traveled. She was unfamiliar with Southport, and the ride here had been a twisty one. It was possible, she claimed,

that the crooks had doubled back on their course in order
to confuse her.

"After the show," mused Norgil. "That helps a lot, Miriam.
It means that the show can still go on."

Miriam understood. To Norgil, putting on the show was
almost as important as trapping the crook who was after
Birdley's jewels.

Outside the house, Norgil and Miriam found themselves
in a deserted section of Southport which neither recognized.
The fourth crook had taken the car; their problem was to
find a vehicle that would get them to the theater.

"It won't matter if we're late," declared Norgil, "because
the schedule is off, anyway. If I don't show up in time,
they'll shove those movie shorts in ahead.

"But remember, Miriam, when we get there, not a word
to anybody—not even to Fritz. There's something haywire
about this setup. I don't want to be bothered with other
details while I'm finding out."

DESPITE the grim events that had been passing elsewhere,
all was quiet at the Crescent Theater. Fritz, checking on
everything ten minutes before the act, found Ling Ro all
dressed. He noticed that Norgil was a bit nervous, but hoped
that would pass as soon as the curtain went up.

When it did, a packed house saw the bland-faced magician
bowing his bald-wigged head. Resplendent in his Chinese
mandarin robes, Ling Ro bore no resemblance to Norgil.
His features were inscrutable, thanks to the half-mask above
his yellowed chin.

As the show progressed, there were two assistants who
registered expressions that could have been observed at
close range.

One was Fritz. He knew that something was up, despite
Norgil's statement to Miriam. The act was going faster

than usual, and Fritz couldn't understand why Norgil wanted to finish it in a hurry.

Speeding the Chinese act was bad business, in Fritz's estimation, and the reaction of the audience seemed to prove it. Even the best tricks looked bad when hurried. Assistants were missing their cues; mutters came from the orchestra pit. The whole show was a nightmare for Fritz.

If Fritz had known what Norgil had been through, plus all that lay at stake, he would have understood. There were times, Fritz knew, when even a smooth performer like Norgil could let the act go sour.

The other assistant whose face betrayed him was Herkin. His expression was one of ugly expectation. Tragedy was stalking tonight, and Herkin was to have a part in it.

The paper-tearing routine was coming to its close. Behind the curtains, Fritz inspected the rifles of the four Chinese soldiers and doled out the cartridges.

The curtains slid apart. To a funereal Chinese tune, Ling Ro was placed against the wall, holding the plate in front of him. The soldiers loaded their rifles and closed the breeches. They brought the guns to the position of order arms.

Herkin was one of those four soldiers. He was in the wrong position, for he was standing farthest from the footlights. Fritz didn't notice the error; nor did he observe what Herkin did, for Fritz was watching for a cue from across stage.

Sliding one hand beneath his tunic, Herkin produced a long, spike-pointed slug and let it slither down into the muzzle of the rifle.

Fritz raised his sword. The rifles leveled. The sword swept downward, signaling for the fire. The rifles spoke, and with their echoes came a clatter, the smashing of the plate that Ling Ro held.

The magician swayed, and as he collapsed the broken

halves of the plate dropped from his numbed fingers and shattered into fragments on the stage. The spectators were rising from their seats to see the finish of this realistic act. They thought that they were being treated to a superb display of showmanship.

Fritz thought otherwise, however. He shouted for the stagehands to close in. When the curtains slid shut, the assistant threw aside his sword and made a long bound across the stage.

The worst had happened.

STOOPED above the fallen form of Ling Ro, Fritz saw that Norgil's scarlet mandarin robe had taken on a deeper crimson dye. From the magician's breast projected the blunt end of the spiked missile that Herkin had inserted in the rifle.

The shot had found its mark in the magician's heart.

"He's dead!" gulped Fritz. "Dead! They—they got Norgil—"

Stagehands were drawing Fritz to his feet, gruffly sympathizing over the tragic accident. Those words stirred Fritz. Excitedly, he pointed across the stage.

"This wasn't an accident!" he exlaimed. "One of those four did it—"

Fritz halted. There were no longer four Chinese soldiers. One of the number had deserted; he was making a quick slide for the stage door.

"It's Herkin!" shouted Fritz. "Grab him!"

They went after Herkin in a disorganized chase that ended as abruptly as it had begun. Coming out into the alley, Fritz and three other unarmed pursuers ran squarely into a parked coupe. Herkin had left that car there; he was at the wheel, thrusting a revolver through the open window on his left.

"There's slugs in this gat, too," snarled Herkin. "Get

back where you came from, mugs, or I'll give you what I handed to Norgil!"

Slowly, Fritz and the others backed away. They were helpless; and Herkin knew that there wasn't a gun backstage. Even the rifles wouldn't do to halt the killer's getaway, because there were no slugs available to drop into the muzzles.

Fritz was the last man to retreat through the stage door. He retired reluctantly, his eyes fixed on Herkin. Fritz's face showed that he wanted vengeance for Norgil's death. Herkin saw that, despite Fritz's Chinese makeup.

Fritz, too, noted Herkin's expression, with its malice. What Fritz didn't see was the crouching figure that approached the coupe from the other side. The sudden challenge that Fritz gave was therefore an unwise one, since he knew of no one who could aid him. In fact, Fritz's action was seemingly suicidal.

Springing suddenly from the stage door, Fritz drove for the car. Men tried to hold him back, for they expected Herkin's gun to blast. Instead, the crook's revolver stayed strangely silent. His fingers seemed to freeze, then open against their will as they let the revolver clatter to the cobblestones of the alley.

Fritz yanked open the door. He didn't have to haul Herkin from the car. The murderer came of his own accord, hands upraised. That was when Fritz first realized that someone had entered the coupe from the other side to press a timely gun muzzle against Herkin's neck.

Gun and hand came into the light; then a face behind them. That was when Fritz's eyes opened to a wideness that almost matched the drop of his jaw.

Murder had been revoked, by a person whose arrival here seemed more marvelous than any of his famed wizardry on the stage.

Herkin's captor was Norgil!

Chapter V
CROSSED CRIME

LIKE OTHERS who saw Norgil, Fritz jumped to one conclusion, incredible though it was. He thought that the magician had somehow escaped a fatal wound, and had risen from where he lay. But that didn't account for Norgil's lack of Chinese costume, nor did it explain how he could have reached the alley without going through the stage door.

A different answer revealed itself when they returned to the stage. There lay the body of dead Ling Ro, precisely as Fritz had viewed it.

Norgil plucked away the top of the murdered man's wig, mask and all. A leathery face came into sight, its eyes opened in a hideous bulge.

"Recognize him, Fritz?"

Fritz shook his head in response to Norgil's query.

"No wonder," remarked Norgil. "The last time you saw him, he had whiskers."

"Bela Bey!" ejaculated Fritz, looking closer. "That's who it is! But how—and why—"

Fritz didn't finish his questions. Two men had arrived from the front of the house. One was Reeves, the theater manager; he introduced his companion as Captain Marhew, of the local police force.

"Just the man I want to see," declared Norgil. "Tell me—what do you know about a chap named Claude Darriel?"

It was Reeves who replied.

"Darriel was out front with me," he said. "I left him, to come back here, when I saw that something had gone wrong."

Captain Marhew nodded. He had been with both of them. He remembered, too, that Darriel had started out toward the lobby when they left him.

"Let's go," suggested Norgil. "I know where we'll find him. There's a lot that Darriel can tell us."

THEIR destination was Darriel's office. Through the frosting of the glass-paneled door, they could see that it was dimly lighted. The glow came from an inner corner; against it, the motion of head and arms was visible.

"What's he up to?" whispered Marhew.

"He's opening the safe," returned Norgil in an undertone. "Give him a few minutes more. It will be easier, captain."

The safe door came open, half blocking the light. There were scraping sounds, the thud of a hammer; next, the screechy wrench of pliers. Suddenly a puff occurred, like the fizz of a faulty firecracker. Darriel's screams drowned out that sound.

Captain Marhew smashed the glass panel with his elbow, then reached through to unlock the door. They found Darriel writhing on the floor, clawing at his face. Beside him was the oblong box that Norgil had given him. From it were issuing the last coils of tear gas that the trick contrivance contained.

When they reached the street with Darriel, the prisoner managed to recognize his captors. He blurted the question:

"What do you want me for?"

"For murder," returned Marhew. "Committed by your accomplice, Herkin."

"But there wasn't any murder," panted Darriel, rubbing his arm across his eyes. "There's Norgil—still alive——"

"But another man is dead," inserted Norgil. "And what you just said, Darriel, amounts to the confession that we came here to get."

IT was in his dressing room that Norgil pieced the full story that only he completely understood.

"Someone was after those gems," he explained, "and I suspected that it might be Bela Bey. But I decided to eliminate him when Darriel came into the picture. I didn't fall for the phony talk he gave me about being Birdley's silent partner.

"So I gave Darriel the tear-gas box. I always keep it in my trunk, with the key beside it, as bait for any sneak thieves who might come into the dressing room. I figured the box would be a good test for Darriel."

It had been. Handcuffed in a corner, Darriel was still trying to rub his tear-tormented eyes.

"Darriel was more dangerous than I suspected," admitted Norgil. "He was sure that he had the jewels, and that I was the only person who knew it. So he ordered Herkin to murder me during the bullet-catching trick.

"Herkin went through with it; and when Darriel saw Ling Ro collapse, he headed for the office to get the jewels and dispose of the incriminating box. But what Darriel didn't know—and Herkin likewise—was that I was not playing the part of Ling Ro."

Enlightenment dawned on the faces of the listeners, particularly when Norgil picked up the Chinese wig with its half-mask.

"Bela Bey was crooked, too," concluded Norgil. "Only he played a different sort of game. He had a crew of thugs on hand to snatch me, so that he could come here and look for the jewels.

"He was not only foxy; he was a good actor. To cover his deed, Bela Bey shaved off his beard and took my place as Ling Ro. He hoped to find the gems; but if he didn't, he intended to join his crew later and go through with the job of torturing me into telling where they were."

The rest was Norgil's own story. He told how he had reached the theater after his escape with Miriam. Arriving at the stage door, he had experienced some real amazement at seeing his own act on the stage, with another man playing the part of Ling Ro!

That had been the clue to Bela Bey's game. Norgil had waited for the act to finish, and deal with Bela Bey afterward. The sudden death of the unbearded crook had been the next surprise, but with it had come Norgil's full knowledge of Claude Darriel's game, with Herkin as the crook's accomplice.

From the moment that he had effectively trapped Herkin, Norgil had taken everything into his own complete control. The box that he had given Darriel as a test of the man's honesty had become a snare, to trap a crook who dealt in murder.

CROSSED crime had brought complete disaster to the crooks engaged in it, thanks to the offstage ability of Norgil the magician. The only other matter that concerned the law was the safety of Birdley's jewels. Captain Marhew asked where Norgil had placed them.

"In the trunk," replied Norgil. Then, to Fritz: "They are in the little compartment, pouch and all. Get them."

Fritz fished for the jewels; his face showed sudden alarm. "They're gone—"

"But not far," inserted Norgil. "We shall find them easily enough, because we know the only man who could have taken them."

Norgil led the way to the stage, where the body of Bela Bey awaited the arrival of the coroner. Stooping, Norgil probed deep beneath the mandarin robe. He found a clasp and loosened it, to bring out the hidden belt.

On opening the pouch, Norgil poured the reclaimed jewels into the hands of the police captain.

From the floor, the face of Bela Bey was grinning in

the ugly fashion that the lost beard had so often masked. Even in death, the cunning crook had not lost the leer that so well suited his malicious nature.

It seemed as though the triumph of successful crime had registered upon his features and frozen there. That sight produced Norgil's comment:

"Bela Bey got what he wanted. But with Darriel in the game, he couldn't keep the swag that he had worked so cleverly to get. He didn't have a chance—"

Norgil paused. Resplendent in the scarlet robe of Ling Ro, Bela Bey still looked the part of a Chinese mandarin. That was why Norgil added:

"Not even a Chinaman's chance!"

The Glass Box

Chapter I
NORGIL MAKES NEWS

TODAY, SO THE newspapers announced, Norgil the magician would be buried and the general public was invited to witness his interment.

The news didn't bother Norgil. In fact, it added flavor to the ham and eggs of his eleven o'clock breakfast. Norgil wasn't dead, and didn't expect to be.

Norgil was to be buried alive.

That prospect, which others would have viewed with horror, was part of the day's work to Norgil, particularly when it brought front-page news. The Portville newspapers were talking of nothing else, and tomorrow Norgil's show would open to capacity business.

"A swell stunt," Norgil told Fritz, across the breakfast table. "I said that the public would eat it up, if we had the casket company supply a glass box. I was right."

The chief assistant nodded agreement. Norgil had performed the living burial before, and sometimes wiseacres had argued that the magician wasn't in the box when it was buried. This time there would be no doubt about it.

Norgil would be on view to all through the glass walls of the box. To make it even better, he wasn't going underground; instead, he would be submerged in thirty feet of water, from the middle of the Harbor Bridge.

Norgil was thumbing through the pages of the Portville newspaper, chuckling as he went along. He finally flung the sheet upon the table.

"We've blasted everything else off the front page," said the magician, "Even the crime news. All that's been pushed back to page four."

"What about the guys who murdered the jeweler?" queried Fritz. "Have they traced them yet?"

"No," replied Norgil. "They cleared town with that safe they swiped and must have switched it to another truck, because all the police found was an empty one.

"Tomorrow"—Norgil's eyes had a thoughtful look—"I'm going to cook up a theory that may lead the police to their headquarters. It would be neat to have the cops walk in just when those birds were ready to blow the safe."

Fritz could see the possibilities. What was more, he believed that Norgil could trace the crooks and their swag through some process of deduction. Though he toured the country as a magician, Norgil had frequently demonstrated his ability as a detective.

Norgil ended Fritz's reverie.

"That's for tomorrow!" The magician thwacked his assistant on the back. "Today, I'm being buried. Let's go over to the theater, Fritz, and take a look at my crystal casket."

THE box was standing on sawhorses in the theater lobby, surrounded by a cluster of gawking townsmen who drew back respectfully when they recognized Norgil. It was a large box, wider and higher than a coffin, and it wasn't made entirely of glass.

Actually, it was a skeleton box of metal, with glass panels on all sides. It had been thoroughly tested to make sure that it was watertight. Examining the hinged lid, Norgil was satisfied on that score.

The top edge of the box was heavily stripped with rubber, so that the lid could be clamped tight shut, preventing leakage. Norgil noted also that the box contained a telephone, with a wire to connect it with the bridge.

"That makes it okay, boss," remarked Fritz, pointing to the phone. "If anything goes sour, give me the call. I'll have you up inside a minute."

"You won't be hearing from me," laughed Norgil. Then, in an undertone, he added: "They only want me to stay under for an hour. With all the air that thing holds, I could stick twice that long."

Leaving Fritz in the lobby, Norgil rounded the block and found the alley to the stage door. He observed a long-built, garish sedan parked near the alley and wondered who owned the fancy car.

NORGIL found out when he reached his dressing room. A bulky, broad-faced man was waiting there to meet him. The visitor was adjusting his necktie at the mirror. Norgil could see the glitter of finger rings, matched by the sparkle of an old-fashioned stickpin.

Turning at Norgil's entry, the broad-faced man thrust out a hand, while he gave the magician a gold-toothed smile of greeting.

"I'm Flash Kurner," boomed the big man. "Owner of the Club Royal. You're Norgil, ain't you?"

Norgil nodded as he shook hands. He had heard of "Flash" Kurner and the club the fellow ran. The place had been a big-time gambling joint, until a recent police shakeup. Since then the Club Royal had been running at a heavy loss.

"Thought I'd drop around and give you a friendly steer," confided Flash. "You're making a big mistake pulling this living burial stunt today."

"Just why?" inquired Norgil.

"You're staging it too late in the afternoon," argued Flash. "It will be pretty near dark before you start."

"I've thought of that," admitted Norgil. "But we had to figure on the tide. It doesn't go out until five o'clock. We don't want the box to foul the pilings of the bridge."

"Why don't you do it earlier?" asked Flash. "Drop the box above the bridge, instead of on the harbor side."

Norgil shook his head. The suggestion came too late. He told Flash that the crowd wouldn't be on hand until five o'clock. Flash suggested a postponement until the next day.

"The show opens tomorrow," countered Norgil. "That means we'd have to set it in the morning. Thanks for the advice, Flash, but it just can't be helped. I'm going overboard tonight at five."

FLASH paused at the dressing room door. His gold-toothed grin had faded. Abruptly he asked:

"How much is the Alvin Casket Works paying you for the stunt?"

"Nothing," returned the magician. "They've supplied the box. I'm getting the publicity."

"I'll hand you five hundred bucks"—Flash was pulling a big roll from his pocket—"if you tell them it's all off."

Norgil shook his head. Flash raised the offer to a thousand dollars. By that time, he saw a clenching of Norgil's fists, a tightening of the lips beneath the magician's trim mustache.

Flash shoved the money back into his pocket.

"Forget it," he gruffed. "No offense meant. I just didn't want to see old man Alvin get a lot of free advertising."

Norgil's fists loosened, but his eyes were fixed on Flash's broad face. The gambler explained further.

"Old Alvin is one of the reform bunch," stated Flash. "He helped queer my business when it was running right. I'd like to get back at him, that's all."

"By making me the goat," purred Norgil. There was something harder than velvet behind that smooth tone. "No wonder there's a lot of people in this town who don't like you. Good-bye, Kurner."

Flash took the hint. He left abruptly.

Norgil could hear his footsteps in the alley. The magician listened until he caught the throb of the sedan's motor. That, Norgil hoped, was the last he would hear from Flash Kurner.

By rights, it should be. Flash had made an offer that Norgil had rejected. There should be other ways whereby Flash Kurner could further his feud against Justin P. Alvin, head of the local casket company, without involving Norgil.

But there were other factors in the game that Flash had not mentioned. The plot went deeper—as Norgil was soon to learn.

Chapter II
BURIED ALIVE

THE HARBOR bridge was a low, wobbly structure, built on pilings that had been driven many years before. It crossed a narrow channel that led to a shallow tidal basin near the heart of Portville.

The bridge was only a few hundred feet in length, and

navigation ended below it. From one shore, only a biscuit toss below the bridge, an abandoned pier jutted out into the water. Beyond that lay rocky promontories, then the channel widened into the actual harbor.

It was still daylight at five o'clock, with promise of another hour before dusk. People had lined the shores, for the police were keeping them off the bridge. A privileged few were allowed upon the old pier, and there, Norgil saw a car that he recognized.

It was Flash Kurner's ornate sedan, with four men standing beside it. Flash's bulky form loomed from the little throng on the pier, and Norgil could picture the gambler enjoying a good laugh.

The truck bringing the glass box hadn't shown up from the theater.

Apparently there had been some mistake. Obliging motorcycle cops had scooted around Portville, to bring back word that the truck had gone to the wrong bridge, a few miles on the other side of town. Norgil's hunch was that the mistake had been intentional, and that Flash Kurner had engineered it.

That simply increased the magician's determination to go through with the stunt.

"I'm going down," he told Fritz, as they stared into the muggy, soup-green water, "if we have to wait until midnight. But it won't be long before the truck gets here. Hurry the crew, when it does."

Fritz nodded.

"And when it gets dark," added Norgil, "throw a lot of headlights on the water. Let everybody see me in that box when it's hauled up."

IT was still daylight when the truck arrived, but with little time to spare. Norgil clambered aboard the truck and settled into the box. Fritz inspected the chains and derrick, while others were clamping the lid shut.

Before the box went over, the assistant examined the tight rubber rim and gave Norgil a nod through the glass top. Stretched at ease, Norgil lifted one arm, and then pointed his finger downward.

Immediately the glass box was swaying over the edge of the bridge. As it tilted, the magician saw the swirl of water just beneath. The tide was going out with plenty of power. That helped, for it meant that the box would surely clear the pilings.

There was a twist as the box settled into the water. Norgil could actually feel the tide's pull, but he knew that the heavily weighted box would stay secure when it reached the bottom. All Norgil had to think about was an hour of rest, with slow, careful breathing.

For the moment, he was intrigued by the descent. A surge of engulfing green wallowed over the box as it went below the surface. Sight of the bridge was blotted out, but there was plenty of visibility in the water itself.

Something thudded against the side of the box. Norgil turned his head to see a frightened fish scud away. He could follow the creature's course for some thirty feet, for the water seemed to absorb the fading daylight.

Other fish were in sight; so were big crabs, clawing the water as they dug for the bottom. The whole thing was like an aquarium in reverse, Norgil being the trapped exhibit on display for the benefit of the sea creatures.

The fish didn't appreciate the humor of the thing—nor did Norgil, a minute later.

THE glass box reached the bottom and settled there unevenly. Its foot rested on a blocky, rocklike base; the head of the box tilted downward at thirty degrees.

Sliding toward the head of the box, Norgil felt the splatter of water against his face.

The box was large enough for him to move about. In alarm, the magician came to hands and knees. He felt for the rubber edge beneath the lid, but it was still tight.

The water was pouring in through a multitude of tiny holes that had been drilled in the steel skeleton frame!

It was coming faster than before. Evidently the holes had been temporarily plugged to pass inspection. There had been dirty work aboard that truck during its planned trip to the wrong bridge.

At this rate, it wouldn't be ten minutes before the box was loaded to capacity with water.

Norgil grabbed the telephone and lifted the receiver. There was no answer. He joggled the hook rapidly, but the line was dead. Whoever had planned this crime wasn't allowing Norgil a chance.

Flash Kurner!

The name repeated itself through Norgil's brain as he crawled from the head of the box to the foot, lugging the telephone with him.

Flash Kurner had ordered this trap, surely enough, and Norgil was thinking of more than how to get out of it. He was figuring that if he did get out alive, from that moment onward he would take measures to settle scores with Flash.

IT was dry at the foot of the box, thanks to the high tilt; but the casket was already half filled. Norgil was dripping with water from which he had crawled. More holes had opened. Even at this spot of refuge, he was pelted by a shower from every side.

Staring through the bottom of the box, Norgil looked for the rock which propped it. His sharp grunt came back to him, echoed by the glass walls. Norgil tensed; he could hear his teeth scrape as he gritted them.

He was thinking too much about Flash Kurner. It was a waste of time, for Norgil already knew more than enough about the plotter. To get out—to strike back at Flash— these were his pressing motives.

The bottom of the box was risky, for there wasn't enough space beneath it. The end of the casket offered a chance at self-rescue, provided the casket wasn't fitted with shatter-proof glass.

With all his strength, Norgil swung the telephone against the up-tilted end of the glass box.

The glass didn't shatter. Walling water prevented that. Instead, it cracked, and pressure did the rest. With a long breath, Norgil let himself slide for the lowered end, just before the glass gave inward.

The deluge almost swamped him. His head buried in his arm, the magician could feel the water's overwhelming surge, with chunks of glass battering amid it. Those pieces didn't cut, though, for they were sinking as they reached the water below.

Then Norgil was working upward until his hands gripped the skeleton frame where the glass had been. He paused there, fighting the impulse that made him want to hurry his trip to the surface.

Coolly, Norgil thrust his face to the highest corner inside the box. As reason told him, there was air there, confined like the atmosphere of a diving bell. Norgil breathed steadily, half a dozen times, consuming that slim reserve of precious oxygen.

Then, dipping his head, he gave a long pull with his hands. Lungs filled with air, Norgil shot clear into the muggy water, bound upon a trip of retribution against the man who had tried to murder him.

Chapter III
CROOKS COUNTER

AS A swimmer, Norgil was both skilled and powerful. He was specially trained to covering distance under water, as he needed that ability in many of the escape stunts that he performed.

In fact, it was his experience as an escapist that had enabled him to keep his wits within the glass box. His last long breath was a process that he had employed on other occasions, and he knew how to make the most of it.

Nevertheless, his present swim was torture. He was keeping deep as he swam shoreward. Almost equal to his desire for life was his wish to remain unseen until he reached his objective.

Norgil's eardrums were roaring. He could feel the tug of the tide. He feared that he had missed his mark, but he fought ahead, up to the last few seconds that his lungs could stand. He was letting himself start upward, when a solid post loomed before his open eyes.

Grabbing the post with one arm, Norgil flipped for the surface with his other hand. His head bobbed above the water; blinking, he shook the water from his hair and heaved deep breaths.

The magician had arrived exactly where he wanted to be. He was beneath the old pier that jutted out into the channel. Norgil had fought against the tide better than he had supposed. The result was that he had passed the pier end before swinging against the posts.

As it happened, that was all the better. It was only a short distance to shore, and from this vantage point Norgil was surely safe from observation.

Peering low, the magician watched the bridge. He expected a long vigil, but it didn't come.

THE GLASS BOX   169

Hoisting gear began to grind upon the bridge. They were pulling up the box only a dozen minutes after it had been submerged!

The reason struck Norgil suddenly.

Fritz had found that the telephone was dead. The assistant had immediately suspected that one flaw might mean another. He had given orders to haul up the box. Probably Fritz expected criticism from Norgil, because the hour hadn't been completed. But Fritz, who always played things as safe as possible, would be willing to risk it.

WHEN the box came from the water, Norgil heard a horrified shout from the pier above him. The shriek was echoed by the crowd across the channel. Despite the dusk, the box could be plainly seen, a cataract gushing through its open end.

Maybe persons expected to see a dead body slide out amid that torrent, for the spectators were silent after their first massed cry.

When they saw that the box was empty, the crowd joined in a long gasp, mingled with groans. That conveyed the very expression that Norgil wanted to hear.

All witnesses believed that Norgil had wriggled from the box too late; that the tide had carried his dead body farther down the channel, treating it as a freakish plaything to hold in its hungry maw.

A self-starter grated sharply upon the pier. There was the whine of a car in reverse. Between the pier posts, Norgil was swimming the short distance to shore. He emerged and took to a clump of bushes.

Luck came his way. The car—Kurner's big sedan—backed in his direction. Its bumper scraped the bushes while Flash and men with him took a last stare to see the hoisted box reach the bridge.

Norgil grabbed for the trunk handle; finding it unlocked, he lifted the back. He rolled inside just as the car started. A quick yank at the clamp and the back descended, to be stopped by the magician's projecting foot.

Having escaped from one predicament, Norgil wasn't looking forward to another. All during the ride that followed, he kept the trunk back open a few inches, pressing it tightly to prevent its rattles.

The big car halted. Norgil could hear occupants alight. He waited a few minutes, then slowly lifted the back. Out of hiding, he closed the trunk quietly. Sneaking away, Norgil saw the wisdom of his precaution. Flash had left one man at the wheel of the car.

THE sedan was pulled up just past the alley leading to the stage entrance of the theater. Norgil could see a light beyond the frosted windows of his own dressing room. Unspotted by the watcher in the car, Norgil reached the stage door.

Once inside, he listened outside the door which stood ajar. Through the crack, he could see Flash Kurner ordering two helpers to pick out articles of clothing and odd objects that belonged to the magician.

Flash's thuggish aids were muttering that they couldn't figure what it was all about.

"They'll be dragging the channel, won't they?" demanded Flash savagely. "Sure. What's more, they'll be working up from the harbor toward the bridge, because everybody figures the tide dragged the body with it.

"If they find the body in a hurry, we won't have to worry. But if they don't"—Flash inserted a descriptive oath, defining the searchers—"we'll have to find one for them. We can't let them fiddle around too long."

With that, Flash turned and clumped toward the door.

Norgil eased toward a spiral stairway leading up to other dressing rooms. He was at the top when Flash's two men joined the big shot.

For the first time, Flash noted the balcony above. It was dim in the backstage darkness.

"Get up there, Leo!" ordered Flash. "Take a gander and see if anybody is around."

Norgil edged to a corner by the spiral steps, to let Leo pass. Nearing the top, the fellow blinked a flashlight. The beam showed the magician's face. Leo gulped.

"There's a guy here!" he throated. "And he's——"

THE rest was lost. Norgil took a grip on Leo's neck. They writhed toward the rail; as they hit it, Leo tried to land a slug. Norgil hoisted the thug over the rail and let go.

As Leo's body made a crackly landing, Norgil sped down the stairs. Flash heard him and flashed a light, but his direction was wrong. Norgil was racing across the stage when Flash finally placed the beam and opened fire with a hastily drawn gun.

Flash didn't have a chance to recognize his quarry. Norgil took a dive as the big shot fired; a gaping stretch of blackness swallowed the racing man from view. When Flash arrived, he found the reason.

There was a trapdoor open in the center of the stage. Its depths had been the fugitive's landing place. Flash swung the light downward, saw nothing but concrete and piled-up boxes. He figured that the fleeing man had crawled helplessly to cover.

That guess was right. But Flash figured, also, that it would be dangerous to waste time around the theater. If the shots had been heard, they might bring a search. Flash added to that opinion when he rejoined the thug who was bending over Leo.

"Chances are I clipped the boob," the big shot boasted. "Anyway, he took a tumble. He can't make trouble. Even if he was up on the balcony, he couldn't have got wise to who we were. How's Leo?"

"Croaked," returned the thug. "His neck's broke."

"Too bad," voiced Flash. Then: "Well, we can still use him. It's going to save time finding the body. Let's go."

Together, Flash and his pal lugged Leo's corpse from the stage door. The rumble of the sedan could be heard backstage; then all was still. Not a sound came from the open trap that yawned in the midst of all that hush.

Maybe Flash Kurner was right in his guess that there would be no trouble from the man who had plunged from sight. On that chance, the big shot had been wise in wasting no more time.

But had Flash guessed that the vanished man had been Norgil the magician, the big shot would have spared no effort to find exactly where the fugitive lay.

Norgil's strategy back at the pier had served him even at the theater, by preserving the illusion that he was lost in seaweed at the bottom of the channel!

Chapter IV
THE SECOND CORPSE

FLASH KURNER had pictured the exact situation regarding the dragging of the channel. Dozens of volunteer searchers were at work in the gathered darkness, using small boats for the hunt.

Bobbing lanterns, sweeping flashlights showed that all had counted on the tide. They were working upward from the rocky promontory that jutted at the harbor's edge.

From the bridge, Fritz and others watched the search. An hour had passed since Norgil's disappearance. It might be morning before the body was found. Faithful Fritz decided to stay on the bridge no matter how long the search required.

Lights glimmered in from the harbor. A larger boat was coming to aid the search. The thing looked like a clumsy scow driven by a chuggy motor. The scow passed the other boats; from its deck, men began to drag on their own line.

No one had noticed that the scow trailed a rope that looked like an anchor line. That sight was lost in the darkness.

The scow had a darkened cabin. In it, a man was seated on heaps of canvas. He kept questioning another man who came in, occasionally, from the deck.

Anyone who knew that low-growled voice would have identified the questioner as Flash Kurner.

"How close are the boats getting?" demanded Flash. It was the tenth time that he had asked the question. "Anywhere near?"

"Pretty close," admitted the informant. "Maybe we can give 'em a quarter hour more."

"Why take a chance?" growled Flash. "Leo has soaked long enough. Haul him up."

The scow was fifty yards from the bridge, approaching the old pier, when a shout arose from its stern. Lights bobbed along the sides. More shouts came, to halt the searchers in other boats.

The body had been found!

WHILE the scow chugged toward the bridge, quick-fingered workers were detaching weights from the corpse that had dragged along at the end of their towline. When flashlights beamed down from the bridge, Fritz and others saw the body, stiff upon the deck.

The chief of police was present. One look told him that the man had not been in the water long. To avoid a curious crowd that gathered, too great for the few police, the chief had the body packed aboard an ambulance.

At the morgue, Fritz got his first good view of the body, and the sight chilled him. The face was mutilated beyond recognition; the marks were terrible gashes that had evidently been caused by chunks of glass.

The dead man's neck was broken, probably by his mad effort at escape when the water swirled inward. That in itself was sufficient cause of death; but the body was also water-logged from its long stay beneath the surface.

All that, at least, was the police theory—and it was enough for Fritz.

The loyal assistant recognized the clothes 'on the body as Norgil's, and there were various papers and other items in the pockets to complete the identification.

Facts regarding Norgil were wanted for the police report. That was why Fritz set out for the theater in the police chief's car. On the way the official did his best to offer consolation.

"There was dirty work that you didn't know about," the chief told Fritz. "I've just learned that a bunch of phony truckers brought that glass box from the theater.

"It looks like they've cleared town, but we'll do our best to locate them. They tampered with the box, all right, but I'd like to know who was behind it. Got any idea?"

Fritz couldn't supply a suggestion. It happened that Norgil hadn't mentioned the interview with Flash Kurner.

"There's been other crimes in Portville," admitted the police chief. "Too many of them recently. The last one was the same as this—murder. That's when they killed Colbury, the jeweler.

"In murdering Colbury, though"—they were stopping

behind the theater, when the police chief added the comment—
"they managed a haul of jewels worth a hundred thousand
dollars. I wonder what they were after, in Norgil's case?"

FRITZ wondered, too. When they entered Norgil's dressing
room, he looked for the few valuables that were kept there,
and found them all in place. Fritz didn't notice that one
of Norgil's suits was missing. The fastidious magician had
a large and ever-changing wardrobe, and many of his suits
were in duplicate.

Thinking over all that the police chief had said, Fritz
didn't hold much hope that the authorities would round
up the culprits. He recalled that the law still had no trail
to either criminals or swag in the jewel robbery.

This case would be a tougher one to crack. It didn't
seem to have a starting point.

There was something solemn about the dressing room.
Fritz noted it as he listlessly dug out papers that the police
chief wanted. No matter where the town might be, Norgil's
dressing room always seemed the same to Fritz.

Time and again, the assistant waited there for the magician's arrival. On this occasion, Fritz's strained ears kept
listening for the familiar footfalls. At times, Fritz thought
he heard them.

Then, suddenly, he was sure of it!

Strange footsteps—draggy, weary—but they had the tread
that Fritz recognized. They sounded outside the dressing room.
The police chief heard them, too, just before they paused.

"It's—it's Norgil!" Fritz was gulping the incredible, and
knew it; but he couldn't hold the words back. "He's come
back—here!"

"Steady, old man." The police chief gripped the assistant's
arm. "A murderer may return to the scene of the crime,
but a dead man never returns."

"But—but Norgil—he's different, and—"

Fritz was going to add the magician sometimes accomplished the incredible; but if anyone's ghost could ever appear, Norgil's would be the first. The police chief silenced him with a gesture.

Stealing to the door, the chief yanked it inward. A figure came through in a long sprawl, to land face-downward. There was a startled cry from Fritz.

Again he recognized Norgil's clothes, damp from the waters of the channel. This was no ghost; it was a solid human form. The police chief thought the same. He stooped close to the prone figure.

"They've pulled too much this time," he blurted. "Swiping a stiff from the morgue and shoving it right under my nose. This is Norgil's body, sure enough."

IT *was* Norgil. They saw that when they rolled the form face-upward. But the face that they viewed brought a startled exclamation from the police chief, a gasp of hope from Fritz.

Though streaked with blood from a forehead gash, the face was intact. It was the real Norgil, at first sight no more than a second corpse returned from the briny channel.

Memory of the footsteps roused Fritz to action. He pressed his hand to Norgil's chest, felt the steady pump of the magician's heart. Assistant and police chief propped Norgil in a chair. By the end of three minutes they revived him from the faint that had followed his painful trip from below stage.

Eyes open, a weary smile upon his lips, Norgil gave his story. That done, he asked what had happened elsewhere. When Fritz recounted the finding of the wrong body, eagerness crept across Norgil's suave features.

The magician's next statement did more than amaze Fritz. It left the assistant speechless, and the police chief mouthing unintelligible gibberish. Out of that mumble the chief formed coherent words as he gripped Norgil's limp hand.

"I'm with you," he declared. "You've done well enough so far. You give the orders from now on."

Norgil's grogginess was ended when he lifted himself from the chair. The police chief's promise could inspire him to any effort.

It meant a settlement with Flash Kurner.

Chapter V
GAMBLER'S CHANCE

FIFTEEN MINUTES found the trio near the old Harbor Bridge, in the police chief's car. The lights were out and in the darkness behind them were other automobiles. The police chief had brought along a large squad, at Norgil's request.

Few automobiles crossed the Harbor Bridge, for a newer highway took more traffic. It happened that a chance car was rolling into sight from the other direction, and Norgil decided to make the most of it.

"Coast down to the old pier," he told the police chief. "You can pick it out easily without headlights. But have that spotlight ready, and post men near the end of the bridge."

The motor was purring as Norgil and Fritz dropped off. Its sound was covered by the car that crossed the bridge. So were the motors of the other police cars that eased from the highway while the police chief was coasting to the pier.

Once on the slope, the chief turned off the ignition. His car was soundless as it rolled out upon the pier, to halt in blackness.

Norgil crept to the shore, followed by Fritz and a detective. They soon found a skiff drawn up among the rocks. It was one of the boats that had helped drag for Norgil's body.

Safely hidden against the blackened waters, they shoved out toward the center of the bridge. Norgil was at the stern of the skiff, using a single oar as a paddle. On his return strokes he sliced the oar through the water, never once lifting it above the surface.

That paddling was more than muffled. It was soundless. There was steel in Norgil's wrists as he kept urging the tiny boat against the tide, until a blackish bulk loomed squarely ahead. They had reached the big scow that had moored beside the bridge.

Men were still aboard the scow. They had waited for the curious throng to leave; then, they had begun operations on their own. Gripping the scow's blunt stern, Norgil and his companions waited, listening to noises that they heard.

THERE were slight splashes beside the scow; next came sharp, eager whispers. Finally the muffled rattle of chains, brought from chunks of canvas. A new voice was heard, low, but commanding in its tone.

Flash Kurner was giving orders.

A winch creaked. It was drawing up the chains. The noise was within ten feet of the stern. It stopped temporarily as an automobile whisked across the bridge. Soon afterward it resumed, with the same caution.

The creak ended. Chains rattled louder, amid muttered words of workers, cut short by Flash's growl. Something thudded the scow's deck in solid style.

Norgil didn't have to give an order of his own. Fritz and the detective were rising with him. As one, they rolled across the scow's high stern like pirates boarding a stricken ship.

But the boarders were not the pirates. This was proven

the moment that Norgil raised a long shout that the police chief awaited.

Instantly, a spotlight burned its shaft from the chief's car. The glare was focused squarely on the scow. It showed half a dozen men spinning in confusion, Flash Kurner in their midst.

Norgil and his companions had the crew covered, but Flash held a gun of his own. Protected by those around him, he tried to use it. Norgil ended that with a long, hard dive to the center of the mass.

Others yanked revolvers. Prompt shots from Fritz and the detective ended their resistance. Some sprawled; others took a dive from the side of the scow. That left Norgil at grips with Flash.

Before Fritz or the detective could reach the pair, pounding footsteps reached the center of the bridge. A wave of police flooded the scow to aid Norgil in his hand-to-hand fight. Like Fritz and the detectives, they weren't needed.

Norgil was astride the prostrate hulk of Flash Kurner, choking the gambler into submission.

Turning the big shot over to the officers, the magician clapped his hand upon the heavy, square-shaped object that the grappling chains had drawn aboard the scow. It was intact, its combination still untouched.

The prize from the channel was the safe that had been stolen when crooks had murdered Colbury, the jeweler!

LATER, at the Portville headquarters, that safe stood open, its contents spread upon the police chief's desk. Colbury's own lists were in the safe; from them the police had made an inventory.

Tiers of jewels were on display in their opened cases, complete to the last gem, with a total value exceeding the estimated hundred thousand dollars.

The only prisoner present to eye that spectacle was Flash Kurner. His mob—some wounded—had been captured without a missing man.

The mystery of the vanished safe stood explained. Flash Kurner, big-shot gambler turned to crime, had shrewdly ordered his workers to drop it from the little-used Harbor Bridge, on the lower side. That explained why the police had found an empty truck outside of town on the night of the robbery.

Norgil took up the story from that point.

"Kurner let one day go by," he told his listeners, "so that he could arrange to get that scow without exciting suspicion. He intended to recover the safe tonight. Today, the papers broke unexpected news about my living burial.

"It wasn't all coincidence. It was a logical choice that made us decide to stage the stunt at the very spot where Flash had dropped the safe overboard. That was why he tried to talk me out of it."

Norgil paused, to study the reactions of the sullen prisoner.

"The idea of a glass box worried him," purred the magician. "He was afraid that I would see the safe, and I did. In fact, the end of the box propped squarely on it—and thereby aided my escape.

"In those moments, I realized that Flash wanted me dead, so that people would look for the crooks who fixed the glass box and forget the channel. That's why I staged my underwater swim."

Norgil didn't have to tell the rest. All knew how Flash had countered, by providing another corpse and having his own men find it. That had ended the search for Norgil, which might eventually have led to a discovery of the submerged safe.

TWO detectives hauled Flash Kurner from his chair. The manacled big shot held them back, to shake both fists at

Norgil. Again the magician noted the comparison between the rings and the ornate stickpin that Flash wore.

Coolly, Norgil interrupted the big shot's fuming oaths with a gesture toward the heaps of gems recovered from the channel.

"You fancied jewelry," purred Norgil. "Maybe that's why you staged the Colbury robbery. You wanted more. You've no kick coming, Flash. You got what you wanted."

The detectives were dragging Flash away. As he went, the big shot rattled the jewelry that Norgil had mentioned. He couldn't deny that the magician had called the turn.

Flash Kurner had acquired bracelets—the handcuffs that would hold him until he reached a murderer's cell.

Battle of Magic

Chapter I
THE WRONG ROAD

ALL ROADS LED to Newbury, scene of the biggest magicians's convention in history. Such, at least, was the claim, but Norgil, ace among magicians, was having trouble finding the right road.

The signposts said Newbury; but the roads were dirt, and they wangled in the wrong direction. The route seemed to be a succession of unmarked detours, carrying Norgil away from his goal. As he turned his coupe along the dirt road that the last sign indicated, Norgil shrugged, and decided that he wouldn't be able to reach Newbury before dark.

Not that it mattered greatly. The big day of the convention wasn't until tomorrow, with the contest show scheduled for the evening. The contest was the thing that interested Norgil, for he was one of the professional magicians slated to appear in it.

A "Battle of Magic" the contest was called; and the term fitted. With twenty-five thousand dollars in cash as the award to the magician performing the cleverest trick, it was no wonder that the best talent in the business would appear, and that tickets for the show had been sold out at premium prices.

Money talked among magicians, even though they claimed they could pluck cash out of thin air. This was to be real money, and the Newbury Convention was the first that had ever offered such an inducement. Usually, magicians worked for little more than traveling expenses at the June conclaves; but this year provided the exception.

The twenty-five-thousand-dollar award was the gift of old Pop Appleby, recently deceased. Wealthiest of all amateur magicians, Old Pop had attended every convention given by the Society of International Magicians, and his will had provided that he should be remembered after he had gone.

Looking for another signpost, Norgil saw something quite as good. A youth was standing near a crossroad, thumbing a hitch-hike. Parked on his other arm was a ventriloquist's dummy that put up a screechy plea for a ride, the moment that the coupe slowed for the crossing.

Recognizing that the youth was an amateur magician, Norgil gave them both a lift, and took the road which pointed to Newbury.

The amateur was about eighteen, with a serious, rounded face. His name was Ronald Halder, and the card that he handed Norgil bore the title "The Great Halder," along with Ronald's picture. The dummy introduced itself as Jerry, and nearly dislocated its wooden jaw in the process.

As he drove along, Norgil kept putting questions, which were answered alternately by "The Great" and his mouthpiece, Jerry. Evidently, The Great felt that he should provide entertainment in return for the ride. Besides, the practice was improving his vent act, which needed it, judging from the way he and the dummy occasionally mixed their voices, by mistake.

The Great was sure that they had taken the wrong road. Plodding along on foot, he had rested by one of the signposts, and was of the opinion that it had been turned. Jerry corroborated The Great's testimony, whereupon Norgil asked:

"Did any other cars come along this road?"

"Yes, sir," replied The Great, respectfully. "An old coupe with a small trailer. It was full, so I didn't try for a hitch."

"Who was in it?"

"A fella and a goil," squawked Jerry, "wid a guy hangin' on de rear."

Norgil stabbed the accelerator so hard that the car seemed to take off across a bump in the road. The Great Halder lost his grip on Jerry, and was too startled to pay any more attention to the dummy. Getting his breath, the youth queried:

"Is there anything wrong, Mr. Norgil?"

"Plenty," gritted Norgil. "The fellow driving the car is Fritz, my chief assistant. The girl is Miriam Laymond, my leading lady. The trailer is carrying my new Dida Illusion."

"The Dida Illusion?"

"Yes. The one where a girl appears in a glass tank, filled with water. I've perfected it so it can be done with a committee surrounding the tank, and they can examine the whole thing before and after. I built the Dida for the contest tomorrow night."

The Great Halder began to understand that the man he had seen riding on the rear of Fritz's car did not belong there. Like Norgil, the youth strained his eyes ahead, looking through the gathering dusk for a sight of the car and trailer that they were trying to overtake.

They saw it, topping the brow of a hill, against the background of the fading sunset. Only half a mile ahead, but the discovery came too late. As Norgil hit the upward, twisty slope at sixty, he gained an angled view that showed him the crouched man on back of Fritz's coupe. From the fellow's position, Norgil knew what he was about. He was loosening the coupling between Fritz's coupe and the two-wheeled trailer that carried the precious Dida Illusion!

Crossing the rise, Norgil and The Great witnessed the catastrophe that followed. The slope on the other side of the hill was steep and straight, but with a sharp turn at the bottom. Applying the brakes, Fritz had negotiated the descent slowly, until lack of pressure from in back told him that the trailer was loose.

Gradually gathering speed, the trailer was overtaking the coupe, and it had become an avalanche on wheels. There was no way to stop its course. Fritz could only hope to get himself and Miriam clear from the juggernaut's path. He did it, in breakneck style.

Giving his old car every ounce of acceleration, Fritz made for the bottom of the hill, outdistancing the wheeled menace that pursued him. The man on the back of Fritz's coupe was clinging tight; he had delayed his jump too long, and had to stick with the car.

From the top of the hill, Norgil's car was joining the mad procession, actually gaining on the unleashed trailer, but with no chance of catching it. Norgil's prey was the marauder who had done the dirty work. He hoped to settle with that fellow, at the bottom of the hill.

Fritz braked his car at the turn below. His old coupe gave a twisty slash on two wheels, righting itself as it took the bend. The trailer kept straight ahead, ripped a rail fence into matchwood, cut a swath through a cornfield, and finished by somersaulting across rough, stony ground.

The trailer mashed itself, together with its cargo, as it took those jack-rabbit bounds. Norgil did not see that crack-up. He was at the bottom of the hill, cutting his speed for the turn. In the gloom ahead, he saw Fritz's car, stopped by the side of the road.

Fritz and Miriam were clambering out from opposite doors, but their passenger was no longer on the back. The fellow was making through the underbrush, to reach a fence that bordered a patch of thinly treed ground. Grabbing a revolver that he always carried on lone tours, Norgil sprang from his car and took up the chase.

The glimmer of dim lights marked a waiting car on a side road. The man who had wrecked the trailer wasn't a lone hand; he had expected this car to pick him up. Shouting for the marauder to stop, Norgil emphasized his command by firing one shot in the air. Instantly, guns began to stab flame from the waiting car.

Flattening, Norgil heard the bullets whine above his head. Those fellows were shooting in earnest, but the magician had dropped low enough to escape the sizzling slugs. Unfortunately, Norgil's position handicapped his own aim. The man who had wrecked the trailer was getting into the waiting car, and it was on the move. Below a slight embankment, the wheels of the car were safe from Norgil's fire.

Unable to puncture the tires or nick the gasoline tank, Norgil simply kept up his own barrage, while the car spurted away, the echoes of its own guns dwindling like the backfires of a faulty motor. Remembering that he had passed the outlet of the side road while coming down the slope, Norgil recognized that pursuit in his own car would be futile.

Returning to the main road, Norgil found Fritz and Miriam listening to details from the combined mouths of The Great Halder and his stooge, Jerry. Norgil cut off the conversation with the suggestion that they take a look at the trailer. They found what was left of it, among boulders beyond the cornfield.

Though battered to a hulk, the trailer was in elegant

condition compared to the Dida Illusion. Constructed mostly
of glass, with thin metal fittings and a platform of plywood,
the Dida was a total loss. The ruin of that fragile apparatus
told the motive beyond the wrecking of the trailer.

It was known that Norgil intended to present a new
illusion in tomorrow's Battle of Magic. It was also generally
conceded that Norgil topped the list of competitors for
the prize award. Someone with an eye upon twenty-five
thousand dollars had arranged this setback, to put Norgil
out of the running.

Who that person was, Norgil intended to learn. Should
he gain the facts he wanted, the town of Newbury would
soon witness a real Battle of Magic, quite different from
the stage show that was scheduled for tomorrow night!

Chapter II
TROUBLE FOR TWO

IT WAS morning, and the main street of Newbury was
alive with people. The town had declared a holiday, and
was making the most of it. From the window of his second-
floor hotel room Norgil studied the scene and smiled.

There were magicians everywhere, doing tricks upon
the slightest provocation. Some were in store windows,
performing sleight of hand; one was catching lighted cigarettes, another was making billiard balls multiply between
his fingertips.

On the sidewalks, other performers were entertaining
with the three-card trick and the shell game. From the
rear seat of an open-topped touring car, an earnest amateur
was clanging away with the linking rings. All this, of course,

was preliminary to the big show scheduled for the evening.

By far the largest crowd was gathered around a ballyhoo platform, farther up the street. There, a sharp-featured man with broad forehead and flowing hair was haranguing the throng in high-pressure style. He was holding envelopes to his broad forehead, shouting the names of playing cards, and giving the numbers of dollar bills, much to the amazement of the multitude.

A voice croaked from Norgil's elbow. It was Jerry, the dummy, parked on the arm of The Great Halder.

"Who's de guy?" was Jerry's query. "De one wid de hair?"

"Count Zeno," replied Norgil. "The mind reader. He's building up his sealed message act, so it will go over big tonight."

Unfolding a list, Norgil showed it to The Great. The list gave the names of performers slated for the evening show. Some were crossed out; others bore question marks. Unmarked, the name of Count Zeno stood out in sorethumb style.

"There's the fellow who thinks he's going to win," purred Norgil. "From things I've heard about the Count, he seldom lets anything block his ambition. He carries stooges when he's on the road; fellows who work as plants in the audience. A hardboiled bunch, but I don't see any of them around today."

The Great listened, open-mouthed; then began to nod. He saw the link. Those missing stooges who traveled with Count Zeno might be the crew that had changed the road signs and wrecked the trailer. The list that Norgil had so carefully winnowed showed that Count Zeno rated higher than the other performers on the bill.

"Zeno is going to stage something special tonight," continued Norgil. "I wish I still had the Dida. However"—he nudged his thumb toward a large suitcase in the corner— "I've got another trick that nobody has ever seen before.

One that even Count Zeno hasn't learned about. I'm going
to use it tonight—"

There was an interruption from the street—the sound of
tom-toms and weird, Oriental flutes. Crowds swarmed to
view the small but strange procession that was approaching
the hotel. First came the musicians, dressed like Hindus;
next a pair of men carrying a stretcher. In the rear were
two others, one lugging a sledgehammer, the other bringing
an anvil.

All attention, however, was centered on the stretcher,
and the man who occupied it. He was dark-skinned, shaggy-
haired, and bearded. His sole garment was a loincloth, made
of a tiger's skin. As for the stretcher, it was a solid board
studded with spikes that pointed upward.

The bearded man was reclining contentedly upon the
spike points. With every jog of the stretcher, he smiled,
and beckoned to the spectators. He had them test the spikes
that fringed the stretcher. The testers were surprised at
the sharpness of the points.

"Yogi Hadra," identified Norgil. "Doing the old fakir
act. He's on the list, but I've crossed him off. The simps
eat up that sort of stuff, but intelligent people know that
it's all hokum. The more spikes, the easier it is, because
it means less weight for each spike."

The stretcher halted just below Norgil's window. The
bearers propped it on legs, like a cot. Yogi Hadra stretched
himself full length upon the spikes; one man laid the anvil
on the fakir's chest. To the amazement of the gawking
crowd, the other assistant began to pound the anvil with
the sledgehammer.

The fellow was husky, and he didn't spare the strokes.
But Yogi Hadra seemed totally unannoyed. In fact, the
only thing that bothered him was a fly that settled on his
forehead. He grimaced as he brushed the insect away; then

leaned his head back, to enjoy the hammer strokes.

Norgil glanced at The Great Halder. The youth's mouth was wide open. So was Jerry's, for The Great had absent-mindedly pulled the cord that worked the dummy's jaw. Norgil couldn't hold back a grin. It was funny, the way people fell for the sledgehammer act. They couldn't seem to realize that the anvil absorbed the shock of the hammer strokes, which were scarcely noticed by the man beneath.

Looking up, Yogi Hadra saw the trio at the window. The fakir grinned, too, and waved a greeting to Norgil. Then, Hadra's face sobered; some important thought had evidently come to him. He gestured for the man to stop hammering. The anvil was removed, and Hadra rose from his spiked couch. An assistant brought a robe; while draping it across his shoulders, Yogi Hadra invited the spectators to examine the spikes.

After lacing sandals to his feet, Yogi Hadra stalked into the hotel. Two minutes later, he had entered Norgil's room and was shaking hands with the magician, while The Great and Jerry viewed the meeting in their open-mouthed fashion.

"I hear you had trouble, Norgil," spoke Yogi Hadra, in dignified style. "Judging from what happened to your trailer, I'd say we were in the same boat. Somebody is trying to put the skids under both of us."

"Your equipment looks all right," returned Norgil, glancing from the window. "What's more, if anybody smashed that bed of spikes, you could make a new one inside half an hour."

"That isn't the trouble," assured Hadra, earnestly. "See those fellows who lugged me along the street? They aren't my regular assistants."

"What happened to the regulars?"

"I don't know. They just didn't show up. I'd been thinking of passing up this crazy contest, and maybe somebody sent them a phony telegram not to come to Newbury."

The situation impressed Norgil. It smacked of his own trouble, the night before. Though Norgil did not consider Yogi Hadra as a strong contestant for the prize, Count Zeno probably did. His own act being largely hokum, Zeno would naturally worry about someone who dealt in a similar line.

Still, Norgil couldn't understand why Hadra needed his regular assistants; at least, not until the yogi undertoned the explanation, after glancing at The Great, to make sure that the youth did not overhear.

"I'm doing the buried-alive act," informed Hadra. "The grave is in the parking lot, next to the theater. They're going to bury me at noon, and dig me up at midnight, when the stage show ends."

"Any chance of a fluke?" asked Norgil.

"That's what worries me," returned Hadra. "I'll have a telephone in the coffin, connected with the police station, and I'm having the storage battery buried with me, so nobody can tamper with it. I can holler for help, if the going gets tough. But if I do, the act will be ruined."

Norgil nodded his understanding. Yogi Hadra gave another glance at The Great; then whispered the remaining details.

"I'm piping the air through a secret tube," he said, "that comes up to a corner of the parking lot. With a car parked over it, nobody will see the tube. But I wanted my own men in the car, to make sure that nobody plugs the pipeline. There's nobody here in Newbury that I can trust; but I figured that you could supply someone."

Norgil agreed that he could. He promised to supply the car as well as the watcher. After a voluble expression of his thanks, Yogi Hadra gave a salaam and departed. From the window, Norgil saw the yogi toss aside his robe and return to his couch of spikes. The procession resumed its parade.

As Yogi Hadra reached the platform where Count Zeno was performing, he signaled for the bearers to pause. On the platform, Zeno stiffened, holding an envelope to his forehead. Hadra's new assistants put on the sledgehammer act, the clang of the anvil drowning Zeno's voice as the mind reader tried to continue with his act.

Judging from the way the crowd flocked about the new attraction, Yogi Hadra was scoring a preliminary victory over Count Zeno. But Hadra wasn't putting on his show for the crowd. He was doing it for Norgil's benefit.

Yogi Hadra was displaying his confidence in Norgil. His eyes toward the distant hotel window, Hadra was telling the watching magician that trouble for two was ended, now that they had combined against a common foe.

But Norgil, remembering the shattered Dida Illusion, was not at all sure that trouble was over.

In Norgil's opinion, trouble had just begun!

Chapter III
THE SHOW GOES ON

THEY BURIED Yogi Hadra at high noon, in a most extravagant and impressive style. The grave was well back in the parking lot, close to the blank wall of the theater. The coffin was a heavy one, of wood, long enough to allow space for the storage battery at the yogi's feet.

Before entering the casket, Yogi Hadra tested the telephone, which was simply a microphone with no receiver. He had to wait for word from the nearby police station, stating that his voice had been heard. That settled, Hadra put himself into a trance, and assistants placed him in the coffin.

There were holes bored in the ends of the long box; small ones, arranged for the passage of the telephone wires, that went underground to police headquarters. There happened to be one hole too many, which seemed a mere oversight on the part of the drillers.

But Norgil knew the reason for the extra hole. It was to admit the pipeline that Yogi Hadra had secretly placed underground, while the telephone wires were being arranged. By the time the coffin had been lowered into the deep grave, and earth was thudding its lid, Norgil could picture the yogi at work, drawing the end of the hidden hose into his cramped wooden dwelling.

It was an hour before the crowd had really dwindled. Norgil remained to the end, lounging beside a parked coupe, where Fritz sat at the wheel. The car was Fritz's; as Norgil had promised, it was directly over the outlet through which Hadra gained his air supply. Fritz was in the know, and was to keep a constant vigil.

"I won't need you until our act goes on," Norgil told Fritz. "Since I'm closing the bill, it will be pretty near midnight, too late for anybody to gum Hadra's stunt. To make sure, though, I'll have The Great relieve you. He's a dependable kid, and can take care of things for the final half hour."

Busy renewing old acquaintances among the visiting professionals, Norgil didn't hunt up The Great until after dinner. By then, The Great and Jerry had become quite the rage of Newbury. They had been doing their act continuously around stores and hotels, and both the youthful ventriloquist and his dummy were husky-voiced when Norgil rescued them.

Norgil took the pair along with him to the committee meeting at the theater. They found three men who formed the prize committee chatting with Herbert Galt, the theater manager. The other performers had left after listing the acts that they intended to do.

Galt was a patient, tired-faced man who evidently had trouble with temperamental magicians, and expected more from Norgil. Galt began with an apology.

"Sorry that you'll have to close the bill," he said. "It's a tough spot, Norgil, but we figured we could hold the audience, if you went on last."

"I wouldn't mind," replied Norgil, "if I still had my Dida Illusion. The trick that I'm going to do instead is pretty small for full stage. However, I'll take the closing spot, if nobody else wants it."

"I'll take it," came a dry voice from the office door. "I'm always glad to help out a fellow performer."

The speaker was Count Zeno. The broad-browed mind reader wore a smirk that belied his helpful offer. His eyes were quick and sharp, as if trying to learn the effect of his words upon all present, including Jerry.

Norgil's own gaze was doubtful. It wasn't in Zeno's makeup to become big-hearted. Norgil gave his acceptance of the offer, however, just so that he could learn the catch behind it.

"Tonight I shall perform an act of super-mentality," announced Zeno, pompously, as he tapped his broad forehead. "I shall ask this committee to write anything they wish upon a sheet of paper and seal it in an envelope. Though the message is written beforehand, away from my presence, I shall reveal it."

Nobody was greatly impressed. Zeno was merely promising to repeat the act that he had performed on the ballyhoo stand. But it happened that the mind reader had more to offer.

There was a small safe in the corner of Galt's office. Its door was open, and its contents were meager. Zeno asked Galt to empty the safe. The theater manager removed some report sheets and pads of passes.

"Who knows the combination of that safe?" Zeno questioned. "That is, beside yourself, Mr. Galt?"

"Only Judge Maulden," replied Galt. "He is my attorney, and occasionally has business here, when I am out of town."

A satisfied smile spread itself on Zeno's lips. Judge Maulden was the most important lawyer in Newbury. He was the executor of the Appleby Estate, and was therefore the man who had charge of the twenty-five thousand dollars that would go to tonight's winner. Mention of Maulden gave Zeno further confidence that he would emerge victor in the Battle of Magic.

"Put the sealed envelope in the safe," Zeno told the committee. "When the safe is brought to the stage, I shall first extract the combination from the brain of Mr. Galt, or Judge Maulden, as you may prefer. I shall open the safe in the presence of the entire audience!"

He put the case dramatically, and the committee men were definitely impressed. Pleased by the way things were going, Count Zeno eyed the safe itself; noting its smallness, he saw a chance to further increase his climax.

"Two men could lift that safe," declared Zeno. "Choose two such men, and before my act goes on, have them carry the safe to any spot within the limits of Newbury. I shall find the safe"—he wagged his finger emphatically—"wherever they have hidden it!"

With that, Count Zeno stalked from the office, leaving the committee in a buzz. They finally decided that Galt and his chauffeur could hide the safe; that when it came to the matter of the combination, Zeno could read the thoughts of Judge Maulden.

The committee wrote their message and sealed it in an envelope. They put the envelope in the safe, and Galt replaced the odds and ends that belonged there. The committee decided that the safe could wait where it was until half an hour before Zeno's act. There would be no reason to inform Judge Maulden of his part, until Count Zeno called him to the stage.

Going back to the hotel, Norgil reviewed the phases of the performance that Zeno was to give. First, the count would have to find the safe, while an expectant audience waited at the theater. It would not take Zeno long, for he was a competent muscle reader. He could get into a car with Galt and the chauffeur and have them drive him around town. Hands resting on their shoulders, Zeno could tell whether he was hot or cold, while searching for the safe.

Getting the combination from Judge Maulden would be easy, too, for Zeno, if he held the judge's arm, and re-peated numbers slowly. Norgil had seen many mind readers perform that stunt; for that matter, Norgil could do it himself.

As for the reading of the message, that was Zeno's regular act. Once Zeno held the envelope, the rest would be easy, for he had several tricky methods of discovering sealed messages, unobserved. But the whole thing would be a grand buildup, with an audience at fever pitch.

No wonder Zeno wanted to close the show! He could foresee himself handing over the envelope with one hand, and receiving the prize money with the other! Meanwhile, Norgil, without his Dida Illusion, would merely be an also-ran among a dozen other performers.

Ruefully, Norgil wished that he could swap places with Yogi Hadra. It would be better to be buried alive, breathing through a hidden air-hose, than to work on the same stage with Count Zeno and see the conceited mind reader win the Battle of Magic by unanimous acclaim. At least, Yogi Hadra wouldn't have to know what happened until it was all over.

THE show began at eight o'clock, and Norgil watched it from out front. The acts were averaging about twenty minutes, and all were good. They were doing their best to win the Battle of Magic, all of these performers.

Norgil wondered how his own act would rate. Without the Dida, he would be just another performer. As the show neared its close, Norgil nudged young Halder, who was seated beside him. The Great followed Norgil outside, bringing Jerry with him. On their way to the parking lot, they saw Galt and his chauffeur loading the theater safe into the trunk of a car, and the sight reminded Norgil that Zeno's act was still to come.

They found Fritz in his coupe. He climbed out, and Norgil told The Great to take his place and stay there until Yogi Hadra was dug up. The Great tried to say something but choked. He gave a swallow and turned to Jerry. Finding his voice, The Great let the dummy use it.

"Aw, chee!" squawked Jerry. "Ain't we goin' to see Norgil do his act?"

"I'll do a special show for you," promised Norgil, "back at the hotel. Right now, I want you fellows to stick here and see that nobody fools around this car."

Accompanied by Fritz, Norgil entered the stage door. There wasn't much apparatus to set; they had it ready, with time to spare. Waiting at the wings, Norgil heard a cool voice beside him; one that spoke with a touch of sarcasm.

"Good luck, Norgil." The speaker was Count Zeno. "I hope you knock them cold."

The orchestra blared for Norgil's entry. The magician strode on stage with Zeno's words echoing in his ears. His teeth gritted, Norgil was wishing the he *could* knock somebody cold.

His opportunity was almost at hand, though Norgil did not realize it!

Chapter IV
CRIME'S TRAIL

NORGIL'S STAGE set consisted of a single, undraped table, and a pack of giant playing cards, four times the size of the usual variety. Norgil showed his skill by shuffling the giant pack; then, at his call, Miriam came on stage, attired in a page's costume.

The girl was bringing a huge goblet; it rang like a bell when Norgil struck it with his wand. He placed the giant pack in the goblet and put the latter on the table.

"You have all seen the rising card trick," Norgil told the audience. "In the familiar version, cards are drawn from the pack, and returned; later, they rise at command. It has long been the magician's dream to cause any card to rise when called for by the audience.

"I intend to perform that marvel, not merely with an ordinary pack, but with these giant cards, which are large enough for all to see the faces. To show that all is fair, I shall withdraw as far as possible; then request someone to call a card at random."

Miriam moved away from one side of the table, while Norgil withdrew to the opposite wing. The audience seemed interested, but no more so than they had been with other acts. Gesturing for silence, Norgil asked for a single person to name a card.

Someone called: "Four of diamonds."

After a few seconds, the four of diamonds began its slow rise from the pack. It was quite effective under the glare of the spotlight, particularly when the card reached the lip of the goblet, and gave a lazy, sideward topple to the floor.

Someone else was calling "Jack of clubs!" but Norgil did not hear it. There were excited voices, just behind him, past the wing. Turning, Norgil saw a white-haired man; knew that he must be Judge Maulden. There was a state trooper, too, who had come in from the stage door. Count Zeno was loitering in the background.

"We must be quite calm," the judge was telling committee men, as Norgil stepped off stage, sensing that something serious had happened. "Mr. Galt has had an accident; they have taken him to the hospital."

"He's unconscious," inserted the state cop, "and his chauffeur is dead. Somebody blasted the bridge over the little creek, just as they were crossing it, coming this way."

Again Judge Maulden advised calmness. Nothing must be done that would start a commotion in the theater. He ordered the committee to watch the show and decide upon the winner.

"The money is here," declared the judge. "I shall produce it in time for the award."

The committee men started out to their places in the audience. Only Norgil remained. A sudden hunch had struck him. He clutched the white-haired man by the arm.

"You say the money is here," exclaimed Norgil. "Do you have it with you, Judge Maulden?"

"Why, no," replied the judge, smiling. "But it is quite secure, and has been, since half-past nine. When I arrived, I went up to Galt's office and locked the twenty-five thousand dollars in his safe."

Norgil wheeled to the state trooper.

"Was there a safe in Galt's car?"

The cop blinked; then shook his head.

"Galt was on the way back!" asserted Norgil. "He'd hidden the safe, with a message in it, for Zeno to find; something you didn't know about, judge! That's why the crooks blasted the bridge. They want the cash; and only Galt or his chauffeur can tell us where the safe is!"

Almost as he finished his statement, Norgil remembered someone else who might help. He wheeled and grabbed Count Zeno. Shaking the long-haired mind reader, Norgil flung him into a chair.

"What do you know about it, Zeno?"

"Nothing . . . nothing!" he chattered. "I can't find the safe—not unless I have Galt—or the other fellow—to lead me——"

"Nobody's going to lead you," interrupted Norgil. "We're going to shove you, Zeno, at the point of a gun!"

Norgil was closing in upon Count Zeno. So was the state cop, and the officer drawing a revolver, inspired by Norgil's suggestion. Seeing himself trapped, Count Zeno showed sudden flight. With a madman's speed, he whipped up the chair and flattened the state trooper with it. Wheeling about, he slashed the wrecked chair at Norgil, landing a glancing blow that staggered the magician.

There was a great roar in Norgil's ears that sounded like the swelling shouts of the audience. Dazedly, he saw Zeno breaking away from stagehands. The count had completed a wild dash through the stage door when Norgil recuperated sufficiently to follow.

Excitement was rising, outside the theater. At the parking lot men were springing into cars, to start for the bridge where Galt's car had been wrecked. Zeno had gotten away, perhaps to a car of his own. People who heard the news were imbued with one idea; to get to the wrecked bridge, and start their hunt for the safe from that point.

Norgil's head wasn't swimming any longer. He spoke to the parking-lot attendant, who was getting his coupe for him. Norgil asked the man if there was another route that led beyond the bridge. The attendant nodded, and gave Norgil brief directions.

Across the lot, Norgil saw Fritz's car. He hurried over and talked to The Great, who was sticking stolidly at his post, despite the hubbub. It was odd, how rapidly thoughts were clicking home to Norgil. Maybe the rap that Zeno had given him with the chair had done something toward improving Norgil's wits.

At any rate, Norgil was piecing facts that he should have recognized before, but hadn't. That was why he told The Great some things that he wanted done. Momentarily, the youth sat bewildered, as if frightened by the possible consequences.

"Talk it over with Jerry," said Norgil, with a grim nudge at the dummy. "He'll tell you it's all right. Then get busy, and don't quit unless the police show up. They'll come, if I'm wrong."

The Great had put Jerry behind the wheel and was climbing out of Fritz's car when Norgil wheeled away. Satisfied that all would work out at the parking lot, Norgil sped for the road beyond the bridge. He struck a point beyond the town limits and began to work inward, knowing that Galt and the chauffeur had planted the safe somewhere within the Newbury area.

Norgil hadn't long to look. Approaching an old, abandoned house, he saw cars parked near it. As he dimmed his own lights, Norgil heard a muffled explosion; saw squirts of flame from the cellar windows of the house. Immediately, figures sprang into a car.

They were wheeling toward Norgil, when he opened a sharp fire and gave them the glare of a spotlight. Finding their route cut off, thinking that the attack meant numbers against them, the crooks swung in the opposite direction, hoping to reach a road near the shattered bridge.

Norgil pursued them. He saw another reason in their eagerness for flight. They had blown the safe; but someone else was rifling it, back at the old house. These fellows were acting as decoys, to take pursuers off the trail. Still,

Norgil followed them, confident that he could make their journey brief.

It proved as short as Norgil hoped. Near the bridge, the crooks were met by a multitude of attackers. Brought by the sounds of gunfire, a dozen men had crossed the shallow creek. They didn't have cars, but they had revolvers, and they raked the mob-manned automobile, when it arrived.

Jerking his coupe to a halt, Norgil sprang in front of the headlights, to let his friends know who he was. After suppressing the crooks in the wrecked car, men reached Norgil on the run. Their leader was the Newbury police chief.

"There's somebody back at the old house," informed Norgil. "Take my car, and you may be able to head him off before he gets away with the cash."

"Count Zeno, huh?" returned the police chief. "The guy's a quick worker. We'll get him, though."

They didn't get Count Zeno. Wading across the creek, Norgil could see the distant headlights along the far road. As he expected, a car pulled away from the old house before the police chief could reach it. From the distance between the cars, Norgil was sure that the man with the swag would make his getaway.

There were taxicabs at the demolished bridge, vehicles that the police had commandeered. Getting into one of the cabs, Norgil told the driver to get him back to the theater in a hurry. They slowed for a traffic light as they neared the parking lot, and Norgil observed that a small crowd had gathered.

It was midnight, the time appointed for digging Yogi Hadra from his self-chosen grave, where he had completed his twelve-hour ordeal. But Norgil wasn't particularly interested in the crowd. He looked for Fritz's car and saw it in its proper corner. He could tell from the vibration that The Great had started the motor, which was all that Norgil needed to know.

Count Zeno could wait. The fugitive mind reader would not do his show tonight. The Battle of Magic had become a real one; and the final act belonged to Norgil, whether on the stage or off!

Chapter V
THE CASH THAT CAME BACK

IT WAS dark below the stage where Norgil waited. It was a place with several exits, easily reached by anyone who had studied its plan beforehand, which Norgil had not. The magician had come in by the only route he knew, through the stage door.

He had heard terrific applause from the audience when he entered, but had not waited to inquire into its cause. Norgil could picture the reason only too well. He had abandoned his own rising-card act, and Count Zeno had fled without attempting to do his mind reading, so it was obvious that the show must be over.

Belowstage, Norgil could still hear the rise and fall of applause, muffled like the roar of a distant jungle beast. He decided that the committee was awarding the prize by acclaim, and that the various performers were stepping on stage in turn, to learn how they had fared.

Evidently, each was liked better than the one before, for each round of applause was more tumultuous. It was fortunate that the sound was muffled, for there was something else that Norgil wanted to hear; something that he was sure would disturb the lower darkness, very soon.

It came—a creeping sound, almost ghostlike. A flashlight twinkled warily; Norgil eased back among some old stage properties, so he wouldn't be observed. The creep became footsteps that reached the wall of the deep cellar. The flashlight showed some dusty scenery that a hand pushed aside.

Then the hand was busy at the bricks. Norgil could see the fingers, as they worked an opening. Both hands were busy, setting a solid section of fastened bricks on a table behind the leaning scenery. The flashlight moved upward; Norgil could see a heave of shoulders, as a figure shoved itself into the opening.

The man was gone when Norgil turned on his flashlight and sprang for the space. As he reached it, a coughing figure came rolling back into the glare. The man wheeled around; his hand plucked a knife from the robe that he was wearing. The blade flashed, coming toward the glitter of the revolver that Norgil shoved into the light.

Above that threatening dirk, Norgil saw the face that he expected—the black-bearded countenance of Yogi Hadra!

Count Zeno's rage had been childish compared to the fury that Yogi Hadra displayed. His hand drove a slashing blow at Norgil that would have carved the magician's face had Hadra's aim been good. But the stroke was wobbly, though it had strength behind it. Missing Norgil's head and shoulder, the knife merely sliced the side of his tuxedo.

Hadra's eyes were rolling. They didn't seem to see the revolver muzzle that Norgil poked between them. Hadra was trying to make another stab when Norgil grabbed his wrist and doubled it. Hearing the blade clatter the cement, Hadra clawed for Norgil's throat. Flinging the revolver aside, Norgil used the same tactics.

Glittering teeth showed between Hadra's bearded lips. The Hindu's coughs increased. He was losing the tussle; his gasps told it. With a final spasm, Yogi Hadra settled limp at Norgil's feet, just as a brilliant light came downward, at an angle, through the space among the bricks.

Looking up, Norgil could see the parking lot, above a deep hole. Men were opening Hadra's coffin, and Norgil could hear their astonished shouts.

"Say—the Hindu is gone!"

"He's down here," called Norgil. "Come on in, some of you, and help me haul him up."

Norgil saw the police chief's face peer over the edge of the opened pit. He gave the chief some added information.

"Look in that battery," said Norgil. "Tell me what you find there, chief."

"Only a couple of dry cells," began the chief. "Wait! There's a package here, too. Say—it's got the cash in it!"

Within the next minute, the chief and the three others reached the cellar, by way of Hadra's empty grave. They found the unconscious Hindu, and began to congratulate Norgil on his victory over so powerful a foe.

"Give the credit to The Great Halder," said Norgil, with a smile. "He did what I told him. He hitched Hadra's air tube to the exhaust of Fritz's car, and pumped the coffin full of gasoline fumes, to soften Hadra when he returned."

There were other details that Norgil gave so rapidly that he left his listeners dumfounded. He told how Hadra had let him in on the "secret" of the air tube, and had asked his help in protecting it. Norgil hadn't guessed the game, at the time.

"He knew I'd suspect that he had a secret outlet," explained Norgil, "unless I thought that he was working the trick some other way. So he bluffed me, with the air-pipe. Those crooks were working for Hadra, not Zeno. He had them smash my trailer, so that I would suspect Zeno, instead.

"Hadra's idea was to steal the cash, not to compete for it. What he needed was an alibi, and he had a perfect one. He had everybody thinking that he was buried alive and couldn't get out. But he had a way out, and he used it.

He must have followed Judge Maulden, and seen him put the cash in the safe. Then Galt and the chauffeur came along and took the safe away. Hadra and his outfit trailed them, and did the rest."

The police chief was nodding. His expression reminded Norgil of Jerry, the dummy. At last, the chief managed to question:

"But what made you suspect Hadra?"

"When Zeno slugged me with the chair," replied Norgil, "I woke up. Zeno went crazy and made a fool of himself. But even that did not change the facts. Zeno didn't have to steal the cash. He was going to win it, and knew it."

Calmly taking the bundle of money from the police chief, Norgil announced that he would give it to the committee and let them pay it to the winner. As he went up to the stairway to the stage, Norgil heard another wave of maddened applause. He couldn't understand it; not until he reached the wing.

Then Norgil stood amazed. The committee wasn't on the stage. All that stood there was a skeleton table, with a big goblet on top of it. The stage was strewn with giant cards, and there was just one card left in the goblet.

The audience was yelling:

"The joker! The joker!"

The last card rose slowly from the glass, wavered over the edge and flipped to the stage, where it landed face up. Norgil saw the card; it was the joker. Miriam came from the other wing, picked up the goblet, and carried it to the footlights.

The applause was terrific. Always a showman, Norgil knew exactly what to do. He bundled the cash beneath his coat; forgot that his garments were torn and dripping, as he nonchalantly came from the wing and took his bow, while receiving the goblet from Miriam.

Between repeated bows and curtain calls, Miriam gave an hysterical explanation of what had happened. Norgil had planned to have five cards rise; no more. Up to that point, Miriam told him, the act had been well received, but was not sensational.

"But you weren't here to end the act," she continued, "and they kept calling for more cards, and more, and more. So the cards kept rising, because—well, because there was nothing else that we could do about it!

"Sometimes cards didn't rise; then people remembered that they'd already risen. It got to be a guessing game, the wildest thing you ever saw. Finally, the only card left was the joker; that's why the whole audience was shouting for it to rise!"

By then, the committee was on the stage, surrounding Norgil, telling him that a vote wasn't necessary to decide upon the winner of the Battle of Magic. Norgil shoveled the bundle of money out through the slit in the side of his coat; the committee took the cash to Judge Maulden, who opened the package in astonishment and handed the money to Norgil.

Long after midnight, Norgil repeated the rising-card act in his hotel room for an enthusiastic audience of two—The Great Halder and Jerry. When the impromptu show was ended, The Great stammered his appreciation; then, finding his poise, he grinned, and let Jerry say:

"Well, I declare! It was quite wonderful, Norgil!"

So was the thing that followed. After taking a portion of the prize money for himself, including the cost of the Dida Illusion, Norgil divided the rest into three and one-half shares. One share for Fritz; another for Miriam; the third for The Great.

The half-share went to Jerry.

THE END

The Magician Norgil, tall and handsome in full evening dress, and Ling Ro, the pantomime Chinese magician, are both anagrams of Loring, the sophisticated stage illusionist who divides his time equally between crimefighting and conjuring. There have been 23 adventures written about him, the first in the November 1937 issue of *Crime Busters,* the last in the November 1940 issue of *Mystery Magazine.* This is the first collection of those tales—and the first collection of stories about a magician detective ever published.

The Author Walter B. Gibson wrote 283 novels about The Shadow, 282 under the Street & Smith house name of Maxwell Grant. He has also written nearly 40 books about magic, both under his own name and as a ghostwriter for Houdini, Thurston and other famous magicians. In addition to books and countless articles on a wide range of subjects, from psychic phenomena to puzzles and sports, he created numerous fictional characters, only two of which appeared in pulp magazines—The Shadow, the most famous pulp creation of them all, and the long forgotten Norgil the Magician, created while Gibson was at the height of his productive powers.

The Artist Steranko's talents are as diverse as they are genuine. As a youngster, he became an expert magician able to perform the type of escapes made famous by Houdini and progressed to dazzling close-up magic and card tricks. He has written the definitive history of the comics, illustrated several comic book series, including *Nick Fury, Agent of S.H.I.E.L.D.* and *Captain America,* created and developed several comic book heroes himself, and recently wrote and illustrated *Chandler,* an innovative pictorial hard-boiled detective thriller. One of the best-known cover and magazine artists in America, he has enhanced the recent paperback series of novels about The Shadow with his pulp-style artwork.

The Publisher The Mysterious Press publishes limited editions of outstanding new books by the world's foremost authors of mystery, crime, suspense, espionage and detective fiction. All books are produced under the editorial direction of Otto Penzler.

A
CATALOG
OF
MYSTERIOUS PRESS
PUBLICATIONS

KEK HUUYGENS, SMUGGLER
by Robert L. Fish
Introduction by the author

This volume collects, for the first time, the complete short stories of one of crime fiction's great crooks—Kek Huuygens, the cleverest and best-paid smuggler ever to outsmart a customs official. By the creator of *Bullitt*, Captain José Da Silva and the incredible Schlock Homes of Bagel Street.

Trade edition, clothbound, pictorial dust wrapper, 156 pages, 1000 copies. $10.00

Limited edition, numbered and signed by Robert L. Fish, in a custom slipcase, 250 copies $20.00

THE KING OF TERRORS
by Robert Bloch
Introduction by the author

Tales of madness and death by the author of *Psycho*. The master of the macabre reveals here his fascination with the dual dreads that threaten the extinction of the ego—insanity and death. Contains 14 stories of sinister terror which creep along the borderline between known horrors and unknown mysteries.

Trade edition, clothbound, pictorial dust wrapper, 202 pages, 1000 copies. $10.00

Limited edition, numbered and signed by Robert Bloch, in a custom slipcase, 250 copies . . . . $20.00 .

Poster
NORGIL THE MAGICIAN

A 20-in. by 26-in. colored poster of Steranko's original frontispiece to this book.

Trade edition, 1000 copies $3.50

Limited edition, numbered and signed by Steranko and Walter B. Gibson/Maxwell Grant, 250 copies $12.50

(Postage and handling $.75 additional for each
order of posters)